"Maalouf is a thoughtful, hun̲ ̲ ̲
interlocutor."
New York Times Book Review

"Amin Maalouf is one of that small handful of writers,
like David Grossman and Ayaan Hirsi Ali, who are
indispensable to us in our current crisis."
New York Times

"Maalouf's fiction offers both a model for the future
and a caution, a way towards cultural understanding
and an appalling measure of the consequences of
failure. His is a voice which Europe cannot afford to
ignore."
The Guardian

"Maalouf writes intriguing novels of exceptional quality."
NRC Handelsblad

"At this time of fundamentalist identity seekers, Amin's
is a voice of wisdom and sanity that sings the complex-
ity and wonder of belonging to many places. He is a
fabulist raconteur; he tells vastly entertaining adventure stories that are also deeply philosophical."
ARIEL DORFMAN, author of *Feeding on Dreams:
Confessions of an Unrepentant Exile*

"Amin Maalouf seems to follow Flaubert in looking at
the East, but he centres the narrative differently: it's
the Orient telling itself. You learn about the multiplicity
of cultures, their openness and permeability; that the

boundaries between religions are not as hard and fast as we've been led to believe."
AAMER HUSSEIN, author of *37 Bridges*

"Amin Maalouf, one of the Arab world's most influential writers, weaves extraordinary tales in his novels, mixing historical events, romantic love, fantasy, and imagination. Yet at the core of all these well-crafted works lies a deep element of philosophical and psychological inquiry into the nature and condition of contemporary man."
American University of Beirut

•

Praise for On the Isle of Antioch

"A marvelous parable."
Le Figaro littéraire

"In this work of speculative fiction, remarkable men lay claim to Ancient Greece and heal an ailing mankind."
L'Obs

"The latest novel of the Franco-Lebanese author isn't just a novel. It's a warning to all passengers: we're moving in a dangerous direction. A cry of alarm, but also of hope."
Le Soir

"One of his most powerful novels."
La Provence

●

Praise for Adrift

"Stunning. ... *Adrift* traces modern events that have resulted in severe geopolitical breakdown, leaving the world 'utterly incapable of marshalling the solidarity necessary to deal with a threat of this magnitude'—the climate emergency."
Globe and Mail

"In a year of pandemic, social breakdown, race riots and, for those in Beirut, exploding ammonium nitrate, you do not have to be a perpetual doomsayer to politely disagree. Now writers do not ask for whom the bell tolls, they simply assume it tolls for everyone and focus on the question: why? One worthy stab at an answer comes from a source underappreciated in Britain—Amin Maalouf, a thinker with a novelist's imagination and a fine understanding of the broad sweep of history ... Maalouf does not offer a clear solution other than the obvious; that we should listen to each other more. He does not preach, and perhaps therein lies our only way forwards to tackle our shared future with the grace and understatement that is the hallmark of his own writing."
The Times

"*Adrift* is so movingly written and so all-encompassing that it would behoove all intelligent humans, and those who are aiming to understand the connections between seemingly disconnected events, to get this book, read it, absorb it and reflect on the ideas the

author puts forward about the collapse of civilizations, the decline of civility and the nature of empires."
New York Journal of Books

"An unavoidably personal and sometimes contentious account, it's born of a post-War liberal worldview which has been unfashionable for some time but still holds much of value."
The Herald Scotland

"*Adrift* is an insightful and profoundly disturbing interpretation of recent world history—and our uncertain future."
The Guardian

"*Adrift* is both an elegy for the Levant in which he grew up, and a reflection on the violent fragmentation and political malaise of globalized capitalism. In Maalouf's portrait, the world in which Covid-19 made its calamitous appearance is disoriented and dangerously unequal, fragmented into identity-based groups, at war with one another yet all beholden to the market."
The London Review of Books

"The writer and scholar delves back into his own history to analyze the tragic consequences of the shock prophesized by Samuel Huntington."
Le Figaro Magazine

"True change is possible: Maalouf shows us possible ways forward in magnificent prose filled with wisdom."
La Provence

"A marvelous, luminous piece of writing."
Europe 1

"Wonderful and terrifying."
La Grande Librairie – France 5

"A powerful voice."
France Culture

"Over rupture and conflict, Amin Maalouf has always preferred epics of encounters, beginnings, and connections."
Le Point

"An alarming report on the state of the world."
Le Soir

•

Praise for The Disoriented

"A thoughtful, philosophically rich story that probes a still-open wound."
Kirkus Reviews

"A powerful and nostalgic current of lost paradise and stolen youth."
Huffington Post

"A great, sensitive testimony on the vulnerability of the individual in an age of global migration."
STEFAN HERTMANS, author of *War and Turpentine* and *The Convert*

"There are novels which reverberate long after you've finished reading them. Amin Maalouf's *The Disoriented* is such a novel. This is a voyage between the Orient and the West, the past and the present, as only the 1993 Goncourt Prize winner knows how to write it."
Le Figaro

"Amin Maalouf gives us a perfect look at the thoughts and feelings that can lead to emigration. One can only be impressed by the magnitude and the precision of his introspection."
Le Monde des Livres

"Maalouf's new book, *The Disoriented*, marks his return to the novel with fanfare. It is a very endearing book."
Lire

"Maalouf makes a rare incursion into the twentieth century, and he evokes his native Lebanon in a state of war, a painful subject which until now he had only touched upon."
Jeune Afrique

"The great virtue of this beautiful novel is that it concedes a human element to war, that it unravels the Lebanese carpet to undo its knots and loosen its strings."
L'Express

"Amin Maalouf has an intact love of Lebanon inside him, as well as ever-enduring suffering and great nostalgia for his youth, which he has perhaps never spoken of as well as he has in this novel."
Page des Libraires

"Full of human warmth and told in an Oriental style, this is a sensitive reflection told through touching portraits."
Notes Bibliographiques

"A great work, which explores the wounds of exile and the compromises of those who stay."
L'Amour des Livres

"What Maalouf discusses in this novel is nothing less than the conflict between the Arab and Western worlds. A personal, honest search for the greatest challenge of current world politics."
De Volkskrant

"Maalouf addresses themes such as multiculturalism, friendship, and disruptive conflict in a pleasant style. *The Disoriented* is a book that enriches readers by providing insight into the memories and facts of life of people from other cultures."
Literair Nederland

"Maalouf manages to drag the reader into a beautiful story that honors friendship and loyalty as essential parts of a decent human existence. He does not judge his characters. No one is completely bad, no one is completely good, all of his characters are recognizable people who are attractive because of their flaws."
De Wereld Morgen

"*The Disoriented* is the new, long-awaited novel by Amin Maalouf, and perhaps his most personal, emotional, and compelling. A novel about memory, friendship, love."
La Compagnia del Mar Rosso

On the Isle of Antioch

Amin Maalouf

On the Isle of Antioch

Translated from the French
by Natasha Lehrer

WORLD EDITIONS
New York

Published in the USA in 2023 by World Editions NY LLC, New York

World Editions
New York

Printed by Lightning Source, USA

World Editions is committed to a sustainable future. Papers used by World Editions meet the FSC standards of certification.

Library of Congress Cataloging in Publication Data is available

ISBN 978-1-64286-134-1

First published as *Nos frères inattendus* in France in 2020 by Editions Grasset & Fasquelle, Paris

This book was published with the support of the CNL.

CNL CENTRE NATIONAL DU LIVRE

Company: worldeditions.org
Facebook: @WorldEditionsInternationalPublishing
Instagram: @WorldEdBooks
TikTok: @worldeditions_tok
Twitter: @WorldEdBooks
YouTube: World Editions

"Novels arise out of the shortcomings of history."
Novalis, *Fragments*

FIRST NOTEBOOK

"So foul a sky clears not without a storm."
Shakespeare, *King John*

The two-hundred-watt light bulb shivered on the ceiling like a puny church taper and went out.

I held my breath. I was tracing the last line of an illustration in Indian ink. My hand froze then rose slowly to avoid making a smudge.

Outside it was stormy, as forecast. Not a rare occurrence in this season on the Atlantic coast. Rain, wind, lightning. Thunder in the background, rolling from one bolt to the next in a constant rumble.

To begin with I wasn't worried. I wasn't even bothered. My working day was almost over. It must have been half-past seven, or maybe slightly later. The drawing was done. A last look tomorrow morning, a few modifications, my signature, and off I'd send it.

I groped around for the lid of my pen and closed it to keep the nib from drying out. Then I felt for the radio at the end of the table, a routine motion.

It's always tuned to the same station, Atlantic Wave, broadcast on longwave from Cornwall. Its music selection is rarely disappointing, and every hour it broadcasts a news bulletin that I'd describe as reliable, covering all sorts of important stories from around the world, not just the feats of the Truro rugby team.

It was exactly what I needed this evening. Convivial music to keep me company in the enforced darkness. Followed in ten or twenty-five minutes by news of the rest of the world, read in the clear, reassuring voice of Barbara Greenville.

A whistling from the radio. No music, no Barbara. Just a two-step whistling that grew louder then died away, like an alarm signal. It wasn't shrill though. Soporific, I'd call it ... I patiently scanned the whole LW band, then MW, then FM. Everywhere this whistling, unwavering, as if all the radio waves had merged into one.

Was the radio broken? I took down an electric torch from the shelf above my head to light the way to my bedroom, where I had another radio by the bed. An older, heavier one. I switched it on. The same whistling. I fiddled with some buttons in a perfunctory way. No, it wasn't broken. I ought to have realized right away. A radio either works or it goes dead when the batteries are flat. At a pinch, if it's had a knock, it might emit a continuous buzzing. Not this regular whistling. Anyway, I was quite sure, no two radios would break down at exactly the same time in exactly the same way.

But then what was it? What was going on?

Suddenly I got it. At least I thought I did.

I collapsed onto the bed, clutching my head.

My God! Is it possible they could have done such a thing?

The bastards! The madmen!

I must have repeated it ten times in a row, "The bastards! The madmen!"—under my breath, out loud. Then I sat up. I held my cellphone in the palm of my hand, with no idea who to call. My goddaughter, perhaps, Adrienne, who lives in Paris ... No network, obviously. The landline was dead as well.

Four or five hours went by, the same words going through my head.

The bastards! The madmen! They dared do such a thing!

Because, as I write these words, I have reason to believe that a tragedy has taken place. Not a natural disaster, but a violent apocalypse shaped by human hands. The ultimate blow to our species. Bringing to an end thousands of years of history. Making the curtain fall on our ancient civilizations. And, incidentally, causing us all to die. This evening. Or maybe tomorrow morning.

I've just gone back over what I wrote. I'm shaking my head with fear and incredulity. Never would I have imagined being able to record such an abomination in an almost steady hand.

What's helping me cope a little, aside from fury, is that it's still unclear what has happened. I'm hoping the next few hours will prove my intuition wrong. But it's true that the events of recent weeks, for anyone who's been following them, have led me to fear the worst. It's also true that all the various malfunctions don't presage anything positive. Not so much the power cut, which isn't unusual when there's bad weather; nor the cellphone network not working, since it always functions fairly erratically here; not even the interruption of radio broadcasts. It's the fact of everything breaking down simultaneously. Just a coincidence? It's hard to believe.

Right now, I don't feel capable of organizing my thoughts or putting together a number of different theories. I can barely describe what I can or can't hear anymore, what I can or can't see, what I'm feeling, nor the recollections that are so rattling me.

*

I've been lying on my bed for a while in the inky darkness. By my ear, the silent cellphone; on the radio, the rhythmic whistling. Outside, the storm has died down a little. The rain's no longer drumming against the roof tiles and the window, which the night has transformed into a tinted mirror.

Out of the blue, I feel the urge to talk to someone. More than an urge, a pressing need. As if my solitude has begun to weigh physically on my chest. And for the first time in twelve years, I slightly regret not living in a town or a village like an ordinary mortal.

The thing is, I live on an island. A tiny island, the smallest of an archipelago of four called the Chirons.

The rest of the population lives on Gros-Chiron, which has the only urban area worthy of the name, Port-Atlantique. The largest island, Fort-Chiron, has been a French naval base for three centuries. I've never been there. Val-Chiron is a natural marine and ornithological reserve, and the only people who spend time there are scientists. My island, the smallest of them all, is called, curiously enough, Antioch.

For a long time I believed I owned the entire island. I'm a little ashamed to talk about that now, what with everything that's going on. But if these pages are to stand as a final testimony, and if someone is to read them one day, I owe it to myself to say something here about my life: my origins, my journey, the solitary existence I chose ... and how it came to be that I now have a neighbor, a novelist named Ève.

*

I was born in Montreal, son of an American mother and a Canadian father who revered his French origins. As a young officer during the Second World War, he took part in the Normandy landings, as did thousands of other Canadians, though for him it was more meaningful. Researching his forebears, he'd discovered they were originally from here, the Chirons, and that they'd set sail from Port-Atlantique three centuries before. To return to "his" land as a liberator was to him the most beautiful recompense.

Several months after the landings, he requested a few days' leave to visit the archipelago. I picture him there, a mustachioed giant, deceptively British-looking, touching and sniffing everything around him, tears pouring down his cheeks.

He was brought over to Antioch. The distinctive characteristic of this tiny island is that it's linked to Gros-Chiron by a causeway called the Gouay that is submerged at high tide but accessible at low tide, meaning that twice a day it can be crossed on foot.

Under the sway of the island's charms, my father was surprised to discover that the local authorities had recently put Antioch up for sale. Since he had the means, and was what you might call impulsive, he promptly purchased the whole thing, then announced solemnly that he would come back before long to build a house on the island and set up home there.

He was unable to keep his promise. In the aftermath of the war, the family experienced a series of catastrophic reversals of fortune. My maternal grandfather, an industrialist from Vermont, found himself in financial difficulty, and my father was ruined in turn trying to bail him out. My parents were forced to sell their West Mount house and move into a soulless apartment. My father landed a low-grade office job, which he must have found very tedious because he never talked about it. He became taciturn, secretive; I sensed he was bitter. The only time his expression ever brightened was when he spoke about his island.

Antioch!

He'd sold everything he owned in Canada to pay off his debts, but had held onto his faraway land. He was hoping to put aside a little money so that one day we might cross the Atlantic, he, my mother, and I, to build a house on our island.

This dream occupied my childhood and adolescence, and well beyond. In contrast to city life, with its routines and frustrations, Antioch was our paradise, ours alone. There we would live off the sea, and the fruit of our land.

If it had been up to me, I'd have taken my parents there right away. I'd have sold whatever we still owned, our furniture, half of our clothes, and travelled to the island to build a cabin out of brushwood.

The Swiss Family Robinson solution occasionally tempted my parents, especially my father when he was daydreaming or depressed. But then just as rapidly they'd change their minds again: "You can't live in a house made of twigs on the shores of the North Atlantic, even on a coastline swept by the Gulf Stream." And more importantly, there was my education. I'd have cheerfully dropped out and opted for the adventure. But my parents didn't see things the same way. "If we succeed in getting you into a good university, we'll have bequeathed you something better than wealth," they used to say.

My father never saw Antioch again. He didn't see me graduate either. I was sixteen when he died. He was fifty-seven.

I think what I've done since would have made him happy. I won scholarships to pursue my studies at McGill and Harvard; I studied law, economics, the history of civilizations; I taught for two years in Seattle, Washington State, and worked for three years in an Ottawa law firm. All before discovering I had only one passion and one talent, which was, in time, to become my bread and butter: drawing. I'm called Alexandre, so I took *Alec Zander* as my nom de plume, which required no more than a minimal graphic modification.

My mother, after a rapid decline, died in Montreal twelve years ago. She'd died twice before already: the first time when they left the house in West Mount, the second when she bade farewell to my father. I like to think I brightened her final years, but she was already suffering, and had more attachments "on the other side from life."

The day of her funeral was white, and the ground at the cemetery was frozen. I gazed around the scene, then one by one at each face present—colleagues pressed for time, furtively glancing at their watches; aloof neighbors; long-forgotten cousins. I suddenly felt the urge to see the sun glittering on a companionable sea. I whispered to my deceased parents: "I fulfilled your conventional aspirations with all my degrees. And now I'm going to fulfil your crazy dream."

"Antioch?" My friends smiled. All of them. "You'll stick it out for six weeks max!" Those who were genuinely intrigued began looking it up in atlases and encyclopedias. *Antioch, today Antakya, a town in Turkey, on the Orontes river* ... No, not that one. *Antioch inlet: name given to the strait that separates the Île de Ré from the Île d'Oléron in western France* ... They were getting closer, but this wasn't *my* Antioch, which featured only on the most detailed nautical maps. And—most importantly of all—on the deed of purchase that my father had carefully preserved.

Did I say that my friends had smiled at my plan? I smiled too, in my own way. All right then, watch me! And off I went. On my own, completely and utterly on my own. Equipped with the property deed, some meager savings, and, most fortunately, a not-insignificant source of income: a syndication contract with a range of newspapers. The character I created, "Groom, the stationary globetrotter," has proved enduringly popular since his conception, so much so that last year my drawings were published on the cartoon pages of eighty-two newspapers in North America, Europe, Australia, and elsewhere. According to the terms of my contract, I am to deliver a three-image cartoon strip each day. Of course, I don't send them off daily, but once a fortnight, in bundles of twelve.

I could send out my drawings from New York, Honolulu, or Singapore, what difference would it make? Here on my island, I work more and better. Right now, I probably have complete cartoon strips for the next four months stacked away in a drawer. Which gives me time to do plenty of other things, like the opinion sketches I publish once a week in *Le Moniteur littéraire*.

*

I lived in a hostel in Port-Atlantique for the first year. The time it took for my house to be built.

Even here on the Chiron archipelago people smiled when they heard I genuinely intended to live on Antioch. Once upon a time there was a fishing village on the island, but it was abandoned more than seventy years ago.

All on my own, I changed the status of the island. From uninhabited to inhabited. Population: one.

When I arrived I was convinced I was the island's sole proprietor. Grave mistake! My father had indeed purchased all that had been put up for sale, a little over thirty-eight hectares of a total surface area of forty-six hectares. The municipality had held on to the rest, undecided as to whether to part with it or not.

I suspect it was also because as a matter of principle they didn't want an individual—a foreigner to boot, a subject of Her Majesty—to take ownership of the entire island. As long as part of it was retained, it was only a piece of land being sold rather than a territory that was being ceded.

Presumably that was also the reason no one bothered to inform me seven years ago that the island authorities, in need of money, had decided to sell off the rest. Which was purchased for a high price by a novelist eager for solitude, Ève Saint-Gilles.

I've no idea if this name still rings a bell, as the English say. The book she'd published at the age of twenty-four was deemed a masterpiece. Its title was *The Future Doesn't Live Here Anymore*. Hailed as the torchbearer of a generation divested of ideas, a generation denied even the glorious reason to carry on living, the anticipation of future happiness, Ève Saint-Gilles found herself in the critical headlights. Celebrated, courted, idolized, but also criticized and occasionally savagely vilified, she was forced out of her university post and ended up falling out with all her friends and family. She travelled the world for three years. Wherever she went she was either acclaimed or mercilessly pilloried.

One day, fed up with polemics and peregrinations, she decided it was time to immerse herself once more in her writing. The public was expecting her second book, the one that would consecrate her reputation. It never came. Instead, she began drinking, a lot. There was mention in the gossip columns of cocaine and amphetamines.

I don't know her well enough to know what persuaded her to come and live on "my" island. What I do know is that thirteen years after her first book she still hasn't published a follow-up. I suppose she's working on it. At any rate, she doesn't seem to have any other occupation.

Nor any kind of social life. People on Port-Atlantique know her by name, but few have set eyes on her. The only people who ever go to her house are delivery drivers bringing orders from the grocery, the fishmonger-cum-delicatessen, or the pharmacy, and every so often the plumber, builder, or electrician.

As for me, I paid her a visit once, five years ago, not long after she arrived. I was annoyed with myself for the way I'd cursed when I'd discovered my island was no longer exclusively mine. I thought it my duty as a polite neighbor to welcome the young woman, and tell her that if ever she needed anything ...

I didn't have her phone number, so I turned up without warning one Sunday afternoon around five. I rang the doorbell, waited, rang again. I was about to leave when at last the door opened. My neighbor stood there in a nightgown. At the time, I assumed I'd interrupted a late afternoon nap; later I found out she always got up around six in the evening and went to bed at ten in the morning. A consummate inversion of human habit.

The visit was clearly a disaster from the start, but I tried to get through it as best I could.

"I'm so sorry, I've obviously come at a bad moment. I'll come back another time."

"I wouldn't bother. What was it you wanted, anyway?"

What a charming welcome! I nearly turned on my heels and left without another word. But I preferred to display my patience—how patient I've become since living according to the rhythm of my island! I reeled off a slightly grudging speech:

"Nothing important. My name's Alexandre and I'm your neighbor, I simply wanted to welcome you to the island. That's all."

With a brief nod I summoned my dignity and turned and walked away.

I'd gone at least thirty steps when I heard a muttered phrase from behind that I decided to assume was "Thank you." Then the front door swung smartly closed.

We don't live the same kind of isolation, I thought to myself, endeavoring to keep my cool. She's running away from people, whom she manifestly loathes, while I've withdrawn from the world to observe it with more equanimity. And also, perhaps, that I might better understand and embrace it.

I wasn't angry with her. I preferred to persuade myself she was suffering, struggling through a thicket of problems; I wasn't going to burden her further. God have mercy on her!

As I walked away from her house towards my own property, my feelings grew mellower still. I even began to feel pleased that I had a silent, ghostly, almost nonexistent novelist for a neighbor instead of some unpleasant, intrusive gossip, or a band of smugglers.

But still, to protect my peace of mind, I promised myself never again to set foot on the other side of the island.

Never again? Until now I had unhesitatingly held fast to this wise promise I'd made myself. But this evening, for the first time, I wavered.

Normally, when I'm in a sociable mood I take myself off to the sailors' bar in Port-Atlantique, have a drink or two and a chat and then, both reconciled to the world of my fellow men and with my desire for solitude bolstered, I go back home to hunker down on my island.

There was no question of going there tonight. Port-Atlantique turns in early, the streets taken over by the stray dogs and cats who gather to sniff out the garbage. And anyway, given how wild the sea was, I'd never have managed to get across the Gouay.

So there I was, going round in circles with gnawing unease, telling myself over and over that I was surely one of the only survivors of the catastrophe, that an invisible pall of death was creeping towards me like a fog, that soon it was going to reach me, envelop me in its poison, devour me like the ogres of my childhood, that this night might be my last, that I might never see the sun or the blue sea again, that out there in the immense world were so many other beings also living on borrowed time, tormented by the same dread, weeping or shouting or whispering comforting words as they held each other tight to give themselves the illusion of strength despite the inevitable.

In the face of this, what was the point of reticence, what matter the injured pride of a spurned neighbor?

So I decided to go back and see Ève Saint-Gilles. She must be awake by now; her day will barely have begun. If she greets me frostily again, with a hostile comment, I'll answer with equal hostility, I'll insult her, spit time-honored curses at her—what do I have to lose?

When I was a child, the worst descriptive I ever heard come out of my father's mouth was "rude." Rudeness to him was unpardonable, be it in a person, an act, an attitude, or an utterance. He worshipped courtesy, politeness, grace. I have inherited this, to a fault.

But what does politeness or courtesy mean on a night like this? And what is grace worth in the face of mass death that will turn everyone into fodder for vermin?

Tonight, I decided, I'll be rude if I must. I'll leapfrog propriety and my own self-esteem. I shall go and visit this woman and talk to her, mortal to mortal.

It was still raining. I put on my fake seaman's yellow oilskin, grabbed my most powerful electric torch, the one that looks like a storm lantern, and went out.

*

I reached my neighbor's house and knocked, for the sake of form, turning the doorknob at the same time. A faint glow came from within, which I assumed was from a candle. I pushed open the door, hung up my dripping oilskin, left my rubber boots on the floor by the entrance, switched off the torch, and walked towards the light.

The novelist was sitting cross-legged on an armchair, completely swathed in a large shawl. One hand poked out, reaching straight up like a feather, holding a glass. On the table sat a bottle of whisky and a radio emitting the same whistling sound as mine.

She was looking straight ahead at either the radio, the bottle, her hand, or her glass. She didn't move and showed no sign of having seen me enter. After a long moment she rattled her glass and said, "If you take it with ice, you'd better get a move on. It'll melt pretty soon."

I noticed alongside her one of those little fridges you get in hotel rooms. I walked around her chair and, by the light of the candle, found an upturned glass and some ice cubes, still hard, barely defrosted at all.

"They'll take a while to melt, it's freezing in here."

She murmured in her gravelly smoker's voice, "Electric heaters don't work very well without electricity."

I smiled, and thought I saw her smile too. Evidently, things were less frosty this evening than on my last foray.

I sat down facing her on an identical armchair and sloshed some whisky over the three or four ice cubes in my glass. A silence. Which could have gone on for much longer. In the interest of making conversation, I said, "Have you found out anything?"

"According to my radio, it seems that *wizzuwizzu-wizz*." She imitated the distinctive whistling. I smiled again. It hadn't been such a bad idea to pay a visit to my neighbor, it turned out.

"Are you always this phlegmatic?" I asked with a hint of sarcasm.

"No. Only during nuclear meltdown."

My smile froze. Clearly, what had been to me no more than hypothesis and fear was, as far as she was concerned, fact.

"Do you really think they might have done it?"

She answered without turning to look at me. "Have you ever played beach volleyball? You throw the ball from hand to hand, jump up to reach it, hit it back, dive down to catch it, laugh, shout, charge around like a headless chicken. But sooner or later, like it or not, the ball's going to touch the ground. Crash."

Our ice cubes clinked at the same moment, as we both lifted our glasses to our lips.

"Perhaps we should make a fire."

"If you like," she said. "There's logs and kindling by the chimney and some old newspapers under the table."

Once the fire had caught, I blew out the candle, came back and sat down, then said, more to myself than her, "When I think that such a disaster happened while I was at home, working at my drawing table, suspecting nothing. There must have been massive blasts, huge mushroom clouds—yet I heard and saw nothing. What an awful day, no?"

"Mankind has gotten what it deserves."

I didn't answer for a moment, then shot back a reply. "I know some who don't deserve it."

"I don't."

She had a look in her eyes now that was almost childlike in its cruelty. Which inclined me to avoid genuine discussion and instead to answer cheerfully, "If I look hard enough, there's a few people I'd like to save. Some friends, my goddaughter, a few neighbors."

"Not me. Not friends, family, or goddaughters. As for neighbors ..."

She made an obscene gesture with her hand and arm. Reproachfully, I retorted, "I'd save the islanders if I could. Starting with those on Antioch."

To be honest, I wasn't being sincere. I was teasing, really, gently ribbing my neighbor. But for some reason this hint of kindness hit home. She turned towards me and flashed me a seductive smile, which she hastily wiped from her face, as if it had betrayed her. Then she muttered, almost too quietly to be heard, "It's better to end your life on a friendly note. Even if it is a sham."

Ève Saint-Gilles must have been beautiful once. In fact, I know she was, I've seen old photos of her: glossy auburn hair, a voluptuous décolleté, and a coquettish smile. But bitterness and alcohol have faded her looks prematurely. I'm fifty-three but look, I'm told—flattery aside—no more than forty-five, while she at thirty-seven looks closer to fifty. And yet her eyes, which you might imagine would be dull, continue to sparkle. If only she'd brush her hair, color it, straighten her shoulders, and stick out her bust—provocatively, generously, flirtatiously, whatever—if only she'd ...

In my mind I let myself play the figure straightener, the savior-chevalier. Looking at her, it struck me that my neighbor is not entirely a lost cause. Apart from the fact that tonight we are all irredeemably lost causes.

"I think I'm going to take a pill and go to bed," she announced abruptly.

She uncrossed her legs and switched off the radio, then struck a match and touched it to the wick of the candle.

"If you don't feel up to walking you can sleep on the sofa. It's beginning to warm up in here."

I rose to my feet and set down my glass.

"Thank you, but no. I need to get back to my bed, my room, my bathroom, my old bachelor routine."

"I understand. Another time. If we don't die by tomorrow, come back and see me!"

*

On the way home, I decided to do the same: take a sleeping pill and go to bed. A night like this there was no way I was going to fall asleep otherwise. It's true that the visit had calmed me, and I felt better prepared to face whatever came next. Nonetheless I knew that as soon as I turned out the lights, alone under the covers with the radio whistling beside me, I wouldn't be able to stop images of my entire life, my friends, and most of all my parents from spooling through my mind. I'd be plunged into all the resentments of the past, and I wouldn't be able to sleep a wink.

When I got home the house was freezing. It's heated with oil, and I have enough in reserve to last two winters, but the boiler mechanism needs electricity to switch on and off and on again. In normal times, when there's a protracted power cut, there's a number to call and it gets sorted out quickly. But I can't call now, so I have no choice but to do like my neighbor and make a fire.

It was so lovely and warm by the hearth I couldn't bear to leave the living room to venture into the arctic chill of the bedroom. So I stayed there, quite still, palms and eyes turned towards the flames.

I've written these lines in one go, sitting in a chair in the firelight, leaning my little notebook on a lavishly illustrated coffee table book about Norman Rockwell, as it happens. I have not reread or tidied up my words in any way.

Outside, the rain has stopped. Everything has fallen silent. It's pleasantly warm in here, though the fire has burned down to a carpet of embers.

I haven't even gotten to what's weighing on my mind. But I'm feeling drowsy now, my hand is heavy, my thoughts are growing muddled. It's time to stop writing and give in to sleep. When I wake up I'll decide what to do with these pages: hang on to them, write more, or use them as kindling to light the next fire.

Wednesday, November 10th

I woke up to the radio still emitting the same rhythmic whistling—the very emblem of the drama. I tried the lights, phone, and internet. Still nothing.

I drew up the blinds and saw the storm had died away. Bright sunshine was already drying the leaves and blades of grass. On a black rock at the bottom of the garden perched a seagull. It turned towards me, our eyes met, it didn't move. It's true, I was a long way away.

Was it possible that the cool air could be so deceptive? Could it be that horror lay beyond this expanse of blue? I slid open the glass door and took a deep breath of sea air. I limbered up my legs, and my seagull flew off snootily with a reproachful squawk.

I was surprised how cheerful I felt, given that absolutely nothing, as far I knew, had changed. I have no idea if the oxygen filling my lungs carried particles of death. But there was sunlight: shimmering, balmy sunlight. I stood there, eyes dazzled, relishing the warmth. There was damp grass to be trodden beneath my bare feet. There was the seagull whose squawking I could still hear in the distance—his, or one of his fellows. And there was the Atlantic. It was high tide; the ocean lapped rhythmically against the rocks that bordered my garden. I walked down to the water's edge, impervious to the cold, stripping off my clothes as I went. When I reached the water I bent down and plunged in my face.

I was alive. I was still alive. One more day? One more week? If something bad awaited me, I decided, I would entrust myself to the ocean. Let it take me!

Let it bear me away wherever it saw fit! Let it swallow me up, and never return my body!

I went back to the house feeling much better. I lit the fire and stretched out alongside it, still naked, as though I were sunbathing.

Usually when I get up in the morning, I ask myself what I have to do that day. I itemize, draw up lists on paper and in my head. Like I used to back when I had a regular job. But today I managed not to ask myself the question. Instead, I focused on feeling sensations in that very moment. The sensations in my body, in each zone of my body, in my head. Wet and dry, ice-cold and burning hot, tension, relaxation, effort, tears, laughter, abandon, the soothing and subtle, drowsy numbness I felt by the fire.

I dozed off again, even though I'd only just gotten up.

The second time I woke up I found I had, unfortunately, returned to my manic organizer temperament. I gave myself orders, beating myself up with lashes of "I ought to," "I must," "I should have."

I found my watch and put it on my wrist. It was 2.15 p.m. I consulted the tide chart on the wall. Low tide today was at 4.19 p.m. If I wanted to go over to Port-Atlantique, I'd have to leave straightaway and be back in three hours at most.

I mounted my trusty steed, an old brick-colored bicycle with a wicker basket that I'd strapped onto the back, and rode off towards the Gouay.

The causeway was still glistening with innumerable puddles, but it was no longer completely underwater. I cautiously made my way across. One slip and

I'd end up face first in the water; the spit of land isn't even six meters wide, and it was very muddy in parts. Besides, the Gouay is neither a bridge nor a walkway but a path three nautical miles long, meaning that at certain points you can't see land at all anymore and it feels like you're peddling towards nowhere in the middle of the Atlantic.

When I reached the other bank, I had to steady my feet on terra firma for a few moments before cycling off again towards the port.

The streets were deserted. But the bar where I'm a regular was thronged with people, just like on a non-fishing day.

The place is called La Cap-Hornière, harking back to the era when seafarers from the Chiron Islands set sail for the other side of the world, very occasionally accompanied by a wife, who in such cases would be honored for all eternity with the epithet *Cap-hornière*, or "Cape Horn Dame."

I was lucky enough to have known the last of the line, who died less than ten years ago. Now her grandson holds court behind the bar. On the wall, among the trophies, hang seafaring relics—old logbooks, bottle labels from Valparaíso and Macassar, a striking sepia photograph blown up to life-size of our very own Cape Horn Dame in a long dress, with her captain husband on the bridge. The kind of handsome, stern faces that hark back to the olden days.

Apart from her, no woman ever sets foot in here, even today. The opposite in fact—sailors come here to get away from them. It's a sad story of estrangement and exhaustion that repeats itself generation after generation. The men go off to sea for weeks and months, while the women stay behind, sovereign over their home lives. The men get out of the habit of living with their wives, the women of obeying a husband. When he gets back home, the house has become too constricting. So he takes off. The most intrepid run away forever to foreign climes; most make do with absconding for the day. To prop up the bar at La Cap-Hornière. They come to drink, play cards with other men, and laugh off their bygone fears.

The bar is always pretty gloomy, so the lack of electric light today was barely noticeable. My eyes quickly grew used to it. I recognized faces, shook hands, and even before I'd sat down, questions for the Canadian, as I'm known round here, began flying thick and fast, peppered with the usual cussing. Was it possible that everything had been destroyed, good God, "even Paris," while here on the islands we'd been forgotten? Cripes, why us? And how many days, how many hours, would this respite last?

Obviously I had no answers, all I could do was add my own fears to theirs. Hadn't we all been following the same events and harboring the same fears? We'd all come to the same conclusion, each in our own words and with our own concerns.

"Our women are afraid," old Gautier whispered to me as though in strictest confidence.

He swallowed his saliva and fell silent again. I squinted at my watch. Nearly five. I gulped down my pint of beer—the wise man's ration—and got up to go. I had another visit to make.

It's rare that I go to Port-Atlantique without stopping on the way there or back to see the man known as the ferryman. Once upon a time the ferryman had a small boat to help people travelling between the islands of Antioch and Gros-Chiron when the Gouay was impassable. Nowadays, this municipal employee's sole responsibility is to keep an eye on the isthmus and make sure it doesn't fall into disrepair. But everyone still calls him the ferryman.

I consider it my duty to go and see him, not only because apart from Ève he's my closest neighbor, but also because it's partly due to me that he lives here. Back when Antioch was uninhabited, the job of ferryman had been abolished. A large rusty sign attached with chains blocked the entrance to the Gouay: *Strictly Forbidden to Cross.*

Given they'd had to lift the prohibition when I moved to the island, the authorities, most conscientiously, subsequently deemed it their responsibility to oversee the causeway. However, so as not to put more strain on the meager municipal budget, someone had come up with an ingenious solution: to offer someone the chance to move into the ferryman's old house and tend the adjoining land in exchange for services rendered. Not very demanding services, it has to be said: they only have to keep an eye on the Gouay for the hour before high tide and ensure no one ventures on to it unawares.

Over the course of the last twelve years, I've known five or six ferrymen: a retired policeman; a young couple lured by the free accommodation; two seasoned sailors ... The most recent arrival, a couple of years ago, was a foreigner. Here on the islands they call anyone a foreigner, whether they come from Manila or the mainland. But this ferryman is a genuine foreigner, so to speak. Greek. Well, not quite; he seems to have a complicated mixed heritage and prefers to describe himself as "of distant Greek descent." At any rate his name, Agamemnon, is the most Hellenic there is, though the locals instantly shortened it to Agam.

He's an extraordinary character, the kind of person you would never imagine encountering in a place like this, or taking on such a modest job. An insatiable reader, bursting with knowledge and crackling with intelligence. He and I have built up a strong bond that goes well beyond the polite relationships I had with the ferrymen before him.

*

As I was making my way up the little path that led to the house, I heard him unlatch an upstairs window. I called up to him, "Not a lot of traffic today?"

"A cyclist crossed a couple of hours ago. Another crossing's expected before dark going the other way."

Our first words were always bantering variations on the same theme: the rarity of traffic on the Gouay. Even today we didn't break with our routine.

By the time I'd parked my bicycle alongside his, Agamemnon had come down and was standing at the front door. He's a tall man, with broad shoulders, and features that suggest the purest mixed blood: high cheekbones, sloping eyes, a dark complexion set off by luxuriant light-chestnut, almost dark-blond hair. At first glance he looks like a Celtic sailor chiseled by the sun and the salty wind; the way he dresses, with his faded baseball cap and jacket emblazoned with a gilt anchor, only reinforces that impression. But on closer observation it's impossible to situate him. He could be the fruit of a love affair between Sitting Bull and a Valkyrie.

I'm no more sensitive than anyone else to male beauty, but I have to say the man is very easy on the eye. Once you look at him it's an effort to turn away. Beauty, indeed, but also a certain strangeness.

"I thought I might see you at La Cap-Hornière."

"I was there for a while around noon," he said. "But I didn't stay long. I had some odd jobs that needed doing, things to fix. My radio's out."

I almost responded—but just in time I saw him smile and give a piratical wink.

"Very funny," I said with a sigh. "You still have it in you to laugh."

"Why wouldn't I laugh?"

"With what's going on?"

"What is going on, for goodness' sake? Everyone's walking around with a face like a funeral. This morning in the bar was a proper pity fest. I felt like asking, where is this dead guy you're all weeping over? I can't see him! I suppose now you, too, are going to tell me about the nuclear catastrophe."

"How could we not talk about it?"

He looked at his watch, then up at the sky. "It's time to survey the causeway. Let's go up and sit for ten minutes. I'll open my best bottle. There's no point in keeping it for tomorrow if there isn't going to be a tomorrow!"

Once we'd sat down at the kitchen table, with him facing the large window that looked out onto the isthmus and me facing the other window through which all I could see were the thinning crowns of a few dry elms, Agamemnon calmly began to speak.

"Like everyone, I've been listening to the news a lot over the last few weeks and dreading an escalation. The mysterious explosion in Maryland; the Americans getting it into their heads to 'clean up' all the nuclear warheads that have 'fallen into the wrong hands' all over the globe ... How were they imagining they were going to carry out this clean-up operation? And what about other countries—were they just going to let themselves be disarmed? No doubt about it—we have all the ingredients for a major crisis. But to conclude that a nuclear apocalypse took place last night is simply mad.

"On the other hand, you're about to point out that something has happened. Something serious, extremely serious. And I don't doubt it. The question is what? No one seems to know. The only thing you and I can be sure of is that we're alive, and nothing around here has been destroyed. Instead of feeling miserable we ought to be rejoicing and celebrating, don't you think?"

He filled our glasses. I thanked him and drank to our health. His words did calm my nerves a little, and I was grateful to him. "But how can you be sure we're not just living on borrowed time?" I said. "No electricity, no phone network, everyone's radios malfunctioning in the same way all at the same time. How do you explain that?"

"Everything's always breaking down here on the islands, especially in this season, and no one ever says it's the end of the world! Having said that, I don't want to minimize what's going on. I'm as worried as you are. Strange things are happening that it's not easy to make sense of. But a nuclear catastrophe? Surely not! The idea that the rest of the world has been wiped out and the inhabitants of the Chiron Islands are the only ones to have survived, and now we're waiting for a radioactive cloud to reach us—that makes no sense."

"I hope you're right, Agam. I truly want to believe that not everything has been destroyed. But the question remains: what's going on?"

"Perfect!" he said. "You see, you've abandoned the bad answers for the good questions! That's always a better place to start from."

He looked at his watch.

"I don't want it to seem like I'm getting rid of you, but I won't be comfortable watching you get onto the Gouay in the dark."

The light was indeed already fading. I don't have very good night vision, and soon I wouldn't be able to distinguish between the sea, blue and grey, and the causeway, grey and blue. I threw him a distracted "See you tomorrow!" before getting on my bicycle and cycling off.

On the way home I began whistling the Toreador aria from *Carmen*. Hearing my voice so jaunty, I realized that the trip to the neighboring island had cheered me up. I was still mystified, of course, with lots of unanswered questions. But I was whistling. Whatever one might say, unbearable doubt is better than dreadful certainty.

*

When I got home, I firmly pressed the light switch and then the radio's on/off button; I picked up the receiver of the ancient wall-mounted phone and even uttered a ludicrous "Hello!" Of course, there wasn't the slightest response or sound. Nothing had changed during my brief excursion, apart from my mood.

*

Thanks to the ferryman I've cheered up somewhat; now I'm feeling a qualified optimism and equanimity, so I shall take time for a brief digression and recount the events of the last few weeks.

I've alluded to them more than once, and I probably ought to have expanded on them yesterday. But I couldn't quite work out how to go about it. Ought I to go over the facts, which all my contemporaries already know? Who for? To be honest, I still don't have the answers. I've just decided to stop wondering. I'm simply going to have to trust my instincts and record in a few paragraphs what came to mind the moment my radios fell silent and led me to fear the worst.

I should probably start by recalling that in the last few years the issue of unbridled nuclear proliferation has been obsessively preoccupying political leaders and the public alike. Nuclear fuel, warheads, even entire missiles, as well as engineers, technicians, and military defectors—all circulating around the world in a whirlwind of rumors.

Apparently, a cartel of arms dealers bought three atomic bombs that they're prepared to set off if anyone tries to storm their lair. Is this true, or pure invention? Who is going to venture into the heart of Borneo or the Amazon jungle to find out?

A terrorist commando putting the finishing touches on an explosive device containing radioactive substances was intercepted on a farm on the outskirts of Dresden. The German authorities played it down, insisting it was all exaggeration and speculation, and subsequently the whole affair was buried under a blanket of silence. How much of any of this is true and how much was dreamed up by conspiracy theorists? I have no idea.

More worrying still, and more pressing too: a fanatical rebel warlord, "Marshal" Sardar Sardarov, ruler of a small mountainous province in the Caucasus, appears to have acquired a substantial number of missiles over the last few years that used to belong to the Soviet military, and his entire political and psychological profile suggests he is willing to use them. Who on earth might be able to make him listen to reason?

This is the background to the devastating explosion that Agamemnon alluded to, which took place a few weeks ago in a small town in Maryland and was, presumably, the trigger for what's been going on since yesterday.

On the afternoon of September 26th, in other words a month and a half ago, a powerful blast rang out at Indian Head, a small port on the bank of the Potomac River, some twenty miles from downtown Washington DC. For the first few hours the local authorities were in a state of denial, not daring to put a name to what had just taken place: an actual nuclear explosion. Admittedly it wasn't very powerful, and its scale was limited: the radius of the damage extended over little more than half a mile. Even so, over six hundred people died and thousands of inhabitants of the surrounding areas were wounded or contaminated. There would have been even more victims if the radioactive cloud hadn't been dispersed by a providential west wind. Seeking to pour oil on troubled waters, certain people insisted that the blast had been an "accident," which, in the strictest sense of the term, was true, given that the people operating the device presumably didn't intend it to go off there and then. Up until the last few days, much of the media continued to assert that those responsible for the disaster were young students fascinated by nuclear physics rather than terrorists planning to attack the US capital; a hypothesis that was hard to take seriously, but equally hard to refute, bearing in mind that all the student wizards had been obliterated without trace.

In the immediate aftermath of the explosion, as people began to realize the implications of what had just happened, an intense dread began to materialize throughout America and the rest of the world. A dread that has only been increasing in the weeks since. It's almost as if the whole world, in shock and completely disoriented, has lost its collective mind. One may think that a little over the top, given that for decades people have been conjuring up scenes of this kind in novels and films, not to mention in reports by the so-called intelligence services. We all know that manuals for building such devices, with detailed instructions and illustrations, have been circulating on the internet for years. And yet when the event actually does take place, there's stunned incredulity.

During this horrifying and frightening time, an armed movement no one had ever heard of before sent a video to various media outlets of a masked man claiming responsibility for the blast. Most terrorism experts believe it to be a fake, and that the video is the work of a fantasist. But some sources think it a mistake to rule out an act of terrorism, and that Marshal Sardarov might indeed be behind it. Some boasts made by the Caucasian despot a couple of days after the explosion have been interpreted as an admission of guilt.

The American president had no choice but to act. During an address broadcast around the world—in which it was obvious how terribly weakened he is now from terminal lung cancer—Howard Milton solemnly announced his decision to "clean up" by whatever means necessary every bomb, every warhead, every last gram of plutonium and enriched uranium, lest anything fall into the hands of wayward individuals—not only in the US, but anywhere in the world. This decision was applauded in North America, Australia, and various European countries, but received elsewhere with suspicion and occasionally anger. Particularly in Russia, China, India, and Pakistan, all of whose leaders declared unequivocally that if the Americans dared to go after their installations or weapons arsenals they would not stand idly by.

Everyone—from leaders to mere mortals—was conscious of the exceptional gravity of the situation.

It's true that during the second half of the twentieth century there were crises that gave rise to the fear of nuclear war between the West and the former Soviet Union; but the few fingers that might then have pressed the button of death belonged to hoary old politicians who feared the judgement of history and the terrified faces of their grandchildren.

There's no reason to suppose that a man like Sardarov would feel similar inhibitions. If his finger did tremble as it hovered over the button, it would more likely be from rage, hatred, and murderous insanity. How to bring a maniac like him to his senses? How to defuse him? By disarming him? With threats? Sanctions? Commando operations? Surprise attacks? None of these means could be deployed without serious risk, and everyone, starting with President Milton, feared triggering a devastating escalation. But there was no way the most powerful man on earth could avoid taking some kind of action.

For the last ten days there's been lots of chatter in the media about one or more imminent clean-up operations in the Caucasus and maybe in other parts of the world too, and everyone's been living with the fear that this could trigger a nuclear war. Leading to my spontaneous reaction last night when everything suddenly crashed.

So, has there been an escalation, with armed skirmishes and nuclear explosions? Perhaps. Perhaps not.

Last month I drew my inspiration from this atmosphere of fear for a cartoon published in *Le Moniteur littéraire* and reproduced all over the world. I depicted our noble planet Earth as a hand grenade, with its latitudes and meridians as its striations. Out of the surface of the planet emerges a hand, reaching over to pull out the pin.

I've gotten into the habit of drawing at the bottom of my cartoons alongside my signature *Smart Alec*, a miniature figure in a top hat who copies the drawing and maybe adds a comment, or distances himself from it. That day, my resigned little character simply blocked his ears, as if the only aspect of the explosion he feared was the noise.

*

I stopped in the kitchen for a quick snack of a piece of goat's cheese and my last slice of bread, before setting out on foot along the path that leads to Ève's house.

I knocked three times, same as yesterday, turning the handle to let myself in, then banging the door behind me to announce my presence, the way someone more discreet would have cleared his throat. I walked towards the living room and called out, "Is anyone home?"

My neighbor replied at once, "I'm upstairs, come quickly!"

I glanced around for the stairs then ran up as fast as my legs could carry me. Through an open doorway I saw the flickering light of a candle. It was Ève's bedroom. She was perched on the edge of the bed in a nightgown. It wasn't yet seven o'clock in the evening.

"Listen!"

I listened. I heard a little staccato melody that sounded like it was coming from a music box.

"It's the radio," said my neighbor. "I left it on with the volume turned down. And then I heard this music just as you came in the front door."

I went over to the old transistor, turned up the volume, and tuned the dial to the station I always listen to, Atlantic Wave. The same music was playing. It was as though every radio, having been condemned to broadcasting the whistling, had now merged into one, all now playing the same tune— soothing, a little monotonous and repetitive, but not quite enough to be irritating.

One thing at least I was sure of: I'd never heard the tune before. I wouldn't have forgotten it.

After a few minutes, Ève suggested I take the radio down to the living room and make a fire.

"I suddenly have the stupid urge to put on some makeup and get dressed before I start my day," she said, shooing me out of the bedroom.

Cradling the white radio in my arms like a poodle, I made my way slowly down the stairs.

When Ève came down the music was still playing. I lowered the volume, but not too much, because of the loud crackling of the twigs burning in the fireplace. Like the previous evening, I'd poured myself a whisky—no ice this time, it had all melted now. I was sitting in the same armchair. She sat down in hers. We were starting to settle into a little routine.

"I was in Port-Atlantique this afternoon. I chatted with a few sailors, and later with Agamemnon, the ferryman. I imagine you know him."

"He's been to see me two or three times, on various pretexts. I've always wondered what brought him to live here. A crime he committed? Unrequited love?"

"Maybe he was just looking for solitude, like us, but didn't have the means to buy his own piece of the island. Being the ferryman is a pretty good solution: a house, land to grow vegetables, fishing for food, and plenty of free time to do as he pleases. I think he reads a lot."

"I know, he's actually read my book, if you can believe it. He quoted entire sentences to me by heart." As she spoke, my neighbor pulled a horrified face. I was careful to show neither amusement nor surprise and went on talking as if I hadn't heard.

"He's convinced that none of the things we feared have come to pass. His argument didn't entirely persuade me, but I did leave his house in a much better mood."

"Great!" said Ève with a little shrug, then went on seamlessly, "Is there really no ice left?"

"None whatsoever, I'm afraid. I even stuck my fingers in the tray. Not a chip. Would you like water instead? If I run it for a few seconds it'll be freezing."

"Yes, I would."

As I walked towards the kitchen, the music on the radio stopped suddenly. I turned up the volume. A woman's voice said, "President Howard Milton has addressed the following recorded message to the people of the United States."

A beat of silence, then the hoarse voice of the statesman came on:

My dear fellow citizens,

First of all, let me reassure you: the territory of the Union has been subject to no violent foreign aggression, we have fallen victim to neither death nor destruction.

I wanted to begin with that reassurance because for the

last few hours many alarmist rumors have been circulating. These rumors have undoubtedly been bolstered by the occurrence of unusual phenomena, including internet outages, the interruption of television and radio broadcasts, the disruption of the telephone networks, and malfunctioning electronic equipment. There is every indication that similar incidents have occurred all over the world.

We now have an explanation for these phenomena, but it would be ill-advised at this stage to discuss it publicly. What I can tell you, however, is that contact has been established at the highest level with the people behind these events, who assure us that they bear no ill will towards the United States. I am confident that through this contact, normal service will be restored as soon as possible.

I no longer wish to hide the fact that since yesterday we find ourselves facing an entirely unprecedented situation. But we do so in a spirit of responsibility and confidence. And I have absolute faith that with the prudence, wisdom, and civic sense of all Americans, and in close cooperation with our friends and partners on every continent, we will get through this complicated episode as safely as we have gotten through other critical moments in our history.

I will keep you informed on a regular basis as things progress. Be patient! And be confident. Everything will work out in the end.

God bless you!

God bless the United States of America!

There were three chords of the national anthem, and the announcer spoke again: "You have been listening to the address ..." I turned down the volume and stared into the flames. Ève followed my gaze. "Penny for your thoughts?" she said after a pause.

It was too soon. A thousand pressing questions

were going round and round in my head that I needed to untangle first. "He says something about 'the people behind these events,'" I said, "but he doesn't name them. Who are they? An organization? A government? It all seems very peculiar and opaque. And he says the US has not been attacked, that there's been no death or destruction. And yet it wasn't what you'd call a victory address. Not a word about Sardarov and his cronies, whom he's promised to crack down on. Have they been killed? Disarmed? He doesn't even mention them. And he says nothing about a nuclear attack. Whether it's taken place, or if they managed to avoid it."

On the radio, the music stopped again to announce a repeat of President Milton's address in a few minutes' time.

"Do you by any chance have one of those old-fashioned battery-operated tape recorders?" I asked.

"Oh yes, of course I do," said Ève, sounding exceedingly amused. "It's probably in that big drawer filled with junk over there."

I had no trouble finding it. I checked it was in working order and set it up next to the radio. This time I listened to the speech even more devoutly than the first.

"Do you realize what we've just heard?" Ève said as Milton was bestowing his final blessings. "A surrender! Nothing less than a declaration of surrender."

She deepened her voice to mimic him and, with a ponderous, wheezing delivery, pronounced, "We find ourselves facing an unexpected adversary, who has disrupted our communications and crippled our equipment, thereby paralyzing our armed forces. Since we have no way to resist, instead we shall talk about it, endlessly ... But let us not panic, my fellow Americans, these people mean us no harm!"

I had to admit that this was a plausible interpretation. But not the only one.

"What other possible interpretation is there?" Ève insisted, growing more spirited.

I didn't have an answer to that. My thoughts were all over the place, confused and sluggish. It was time to go. I got to my feet.

"Would you mind lending me the tape recorder till tomorrow? It's the kind of speech you need to listen to several times to figure out what's lurking behind each word."

"You'd be doing me a favor if you got rid of that thing for good; I never want to see it again. I bought it last year thinking it would help me write. Instead of scratching pen to paper or tapping away on a keyboard, I'd just stroll along the beach and speak into the little box. Miracle solution! I wandered around for hours and days on end, microphone to my lips, and never managed to dictate a single sentence. Take it and keep it. At least it'll be useful to someone."

*

Ève had a point; this reference to an adversary whose name Milton failed to disclose is very odd. He doesn't call him an "adversary" or an "enemy" or a "partner." He speaks of him with a kind of timid deference. *It would be ill-advised at this stage to discuss it publicly*, he tells us. A circumspection quite different to the usual style of the most powerful man on earth.

What we'd just heard was not Hernan Cortés telling his people about meeting Moctezuma, but Moctezuma telling his people about his encounter with Cortés.

So, although yesterday's dread has somewhat dissipated, another has taken shape, less concrete, more unquantifiable. There hasn't been a nuclear catastrophe. There's an explanation for what's happened. But something is going on, something major and unanticipated, and with barely any details I am unable to gauge either its magnitude or its implications.

*Thursday, November 11*th

The role of chronicler I've assigned myself turns out to be exhausting. I'm spending all my waking hours waiting for news, verifying facts, taking notes, and writing it all up. At least tonight I'll be writing by the light of my desk lamp.

Because the power's back! When I opened my eyes this morning at around half past ten, all the electric clocks around the house—on the computer, printer, stereo, oven, freezer—were blinking on and off. Red, pink, turquoise, all peeping to me that they weren't telling the right time and wanted to be adjusted.

I picked up the phone and dialed my goddaughter Adrienne's number in Paris. I got a recorded message, but at least it was her voice. The network seems to have been restored. The airwaves are no longer blocked.

My second call was to my oldest friend—or to be precise, the oldest friend with whom I've stayed continuously in touch—Moro. I'll no doubt talk about him again, but I should explain right away why I was so keen to reach him.

We met at university, where he was already something of a legend. Smart and hardworking, with a brilliant sense of humor. That was what first drew me to him. His physical appearance as well, the too-round head and too-frizzy hair against the too-white skin, glasses thick as jewelry-store windows, the wolfish grin of an eager child. Short-sighted and stocky, he didn't exactly correspond to standard notions of beauty; but in the hierarchy of seduction that shrugs off convention he reigned supreme.

We built up the kind of strong bond that isn't affected by time and distance. I'm still in the habit of telling him things I'd never tell anyone else, and he's the same. We haven't seen each other much over the last few years. We've both been doing our own thing: I gave up law to become a cartoonist and left the New World to live on my ancestral island; Moro became a topnotch lawyer, with the most recondite litigation briefs winging their way to him from São Paulo, Toronto, London, and Singapore. He's never lumbered himself with a big law firm bearing his name. He floats around—as he does in matters of the heart as well—according to whatever cases he's working on.

A luminary, then, to his colleagues, and something of a god to his friends. Even so, he stayed out of the spotlight for a long time. Yes, even in a society as flashy as that of the United States, he achieved the feat of becoming important while remaining unknown. And then three years ago, out of the blue, his name and face were revealed to the public. It would have been hard to avoid, given that one of his closest friends had just entered the White House.

I've never met Howard Milton, before or since he became president. It's possible his gaze has occasionally lingered on one of my drawings, but he wouldn't have known who is concealed behind Alec Zander's nom de plume, nor the subterranean kinship that connects us. Moro keeps his friends separate. Even I knew barely anything about their relationship until it became public knowledge.

During the presidential campaign, various newspapers mentioned the name "Morris Oates, a.k.a. Moro," without elaborating on his role. It was only after the election, once the new president's every move began to come under scrutiny twenty-four hours a day, that the truth was revealed. People began talking about a very special adviser, an éminence grise, a confessor, a magician, a guru ... I don't know how Moro's other friends reacted; for my part, I was more annoyed than proud.

That's definitely not the case today. I'd go so far as to say I'm enchanted that one of my friends has been propelled to such dizzying heights. There's massive political turmoil going on, and the media's aphasic. I need to find out what's happening, and he is bound to know.

I dialed his number. It wasn't yet 5 a.m. in Washington—not the most civilized time to call. But with Moro that's never an issue. I know his habits: as long as it doesn't bother him to take a call, he keeps his phone on; if he's getting ready for bed, or concentrating on a case, he switches it off. He has a point. You might be immersed in a piece of work at midday, and a call would be an intolerable intrusion; on the other hand, sometimes you're more than happy to chat with someone in the middle of the night. And how would I even know if my friend was at home rather than in Tokyo, Athens, Sydney, or Kuala Lumpur? Whenever I want to reach him, I never worry about the time zone, I just call.

He picked up on the second ring.

"Alec! You're quick. It's not even been twenty minutes since the network was restored."

"Tell me I'm not disturbing you."

"I'm in Santiago de Chile, it's seven in the morning, I didn't sleep a wink all night. You're not bothering me at all, but the rest of humanity is irritating me in the extreme."

He burst into his boyish chuckle, which banished all thought of passing time and greying temples. A few loud chortles, then he stopped abruptly. The other Moro had something to say. The observer of the world, the analyst of crises, the *very* special adviser. Whose tone manages to be both affable and serious, today more than ever. Who gets straight to the point. Who answers the question before the questioner has even formulated it.

"Something really disturbing has happened. Which we're partly responsible for, though we couldn't have prevented it." He confirmed the rumors that had been circulating in the media the last week, that a cleanup of Marshal Sardarov's stronghold in the Caucasus to neutralize his nuclear arsenal had been in the offing.

"The Russians weren't going to be happy, nor the Chinese, Indians, or Europeans; but after what happened in Maryland, they all knew we had to act and no one contemplated standing in our way. That lunatic Sardarov had practically claimed responsibility for a nuclear attack on US soil. Did he really order it? That's another question. But he bragged about it, which was enough to ensure he wouldn't go unpunished.

"The strike was planned for next week, our military was figuring out the final details. Then on Monday we learned from reliable sources that Sardarov was preparing to launch attacks on several cities. We intercepted a conversation in which he was heard saying, 'If they want to take my rockets, they will have to kill me first. The Soviet Union let itself be defeated and broken up without ever daring to use its weapons. They will not take my missiles intact. I am going to explode the lot of them, and not over the desert or the sea.'

"We were on Air Force One when Howard received an alarming message from the intelligence services: Sardarov was planning to launch an attack within the next twenty-four hours. We'd literally just landed in Santiago, on the beginning of a Latin American tour, and the Pentagon was asking for instructions. We had to decide right away.

"I am sure no enemy missile would have reached us territory; they'd all have been intercepted and destroyed in midair," he went on. "But other targets would have been hit, in Europe, the Middle East, South Asia, which would have caused a major disaster. Could we risk the destruction of cities like Athens, Vienna, Rome, Jerusalem, Istanbul, or Dubai? The president was compelled to act.

"The original plan called for commando operations to seize the Marshal's bases and painstakingly dismantle the warheads. But now the situation had changed, and we had no choice but to destroy the missiles in a massive bombing campaign before they could be fired.

"This was bound to cause devastation in the

Caucasus, in the vicinity of the launch pads, and we were fully aware of this. But what else could we do? Either we destroyed the missiles immediately, leading inevitably to a huge number of deaths, or we ran the risk of the missiles being fired and hitting their targets, leading to even more deaths among our allies. The military was calling for an immediate strike and urging the president to give his approval without further delay.

"The plane was sitting on the tarmac at the airport. Alicia O'Brien, the Chilean president, was waiting at the bottom of the gangway. The US ambassador to Chile had just boarded the plane. I was sitting behind the president. I heard him say, 'I give my consent, you may proceed.' He was silent for a couple of moments, like he was waiting for a 'Thank you!' or a 'Yes!' or a 'Goodbye,' but then he said, 'Hello! Hello!' He turned to his aide. 'My cellphone's not working. Could you call the Secretary of Defense and get him back on the line?' But the aide's cellphone wasn't working either. Nor was mine. Nor the ambassador's. All dead.

"In line with the official program for the visit, Alicia O'Brian accompanied us to the presidential palace, La Moneda, where a reception was being held in Howard's honor. Waiting there for us were local dignitaries, foreign diplomats, and some American citizens living in Chile. When we arrived it was clear that everyone, without exception, was having the same problem with their cellphones. Landlines weren't working either, and computers couldn't connect to the internet. This in and of itself was very concerning, and Howard was beside himself with fury that he had no idea whether or not his authorization to destroy Sardarov's missiles had been received by the Pentagon.

"The plan was for the two heads of state to meet privately, sign various bilateral agreements that had been drawn up, and make their way together to a large reception, where they would give the customary speeches and have a drink with the guests. We entered the president's office. She and Howard sat down. Their respective entourages were about to retire to give them a few minutes alone, when something very odd happened.

"On one of the shelves of the library there was a tablet propped up against some books. No one even noticed it. Who notices screens nowadays? They're everywhere, blending into the background. But suddenly the screen, which had been dark like all the others, lit up, came to life, and a loud voice was heard, 'Good afternoon, Mr. President!'

"Everyone turned to the face on the screen. The security officers were frantic. They thought there had been an attack, or at least some kind of disruptive incursion. Some of them automatically put their cellphones to their ears or held them up to their mouths as if they were walkie-talkies. Then they realized, of course, that they weren't transmitting or receiving anything. The figure on the screen smiled and said, as if he could see them: 'Your cellphones aren't working. I'm here to restore the network.'

"Members of both delegations were now gathered in a circle around the screen, awaiting instructions. And it wasn't long before they got them. This time in Spanish: 'I am right now inside the palace among your guests, Madame President. Perhaps one of your people would care to come and find me and bring me to you.'

"I can't help thinking that if this character had managed to get inside the palace, despite the strict security checks, he could have made his way to the president's office on his own. But he obviously wanted to do things by the book. So one of the Chilean president's staffers was dispatched to find him. Four or five security men accompanied him. We saw the man come in, escorted by this small troupe, a head taller than all of them and sporting the same faint smile as he'd had onscreen.

"A few people looked like they were about to grab him for close questioning. But our president stood up to shake his hand, and then President O'Brien did the same, before inviting him to take a seat.

"'Perhaps you could tell someone to close the door?' the intruder suggested politely. It was he, of course, who was doing the telling.

"There was a flurry of commotion among those present. Should they stay or leave the room? It was Howard who decided for everyone. He instructed four of his staff, including myself, to remain with him. Then President O'Brien appointed four of her people to stay with her. Everybody else left.

"As soon as the door closed, the man turned to Howard. 'Mr. President, two hours ago or thereabouts you gave the order for the bombing of military bases in and around Gaborny. You may rest assured that your order was not transmitted.'

"The president grew even paler. I could tell it was an effort for him to make his voice audible. 'What you are telling me is far from reassuring. I did order the destruction of the missiles that Marshal Sardarov was planning to use to attack multiple cities around the world. I had to take the decision to bomb the bases to avert a major disaster that would have led to the deaths of hundreds of thousands, maybe millions.'

"The other man replied, 'Indeed, Mr. President, what you say is quite true. Sardarov was planning to launch his warhead against several metropolises, with intent to cause as many casualties as possible. You will be reassured to know that he too was unable to transmit his orders, and that his missiles could not be launched. The bombs are out of action. As is the marshal.'

"'Well, that certainly sets my mind at rest,' said Howard. 'I ordered the attack with a heavy heart—it's not as if I was unaware that bombing the launch pads would cause multiple civilian casualties. But if we didn't do it, entire cities were going to be destroyed.'

"'Again, Mr. President, I confirm that with the limited time you had, and the means at your disposal, there was no option other than the one you chose. Which is why we were forced to intervene.'

"There was swagger in his words. And arrogance too. 'Who are you?' Howard asked him. This was obviously the question on everybody's mind. We all watched him with great curiosity. He gave the appearance of being deep in thought, though I'm sure his answer was already prepared, along with the appropriate intonation.

"'Mr. President, your question is legitimate, and I promise to answer it in due course. But right now, you have guests awaiting you, and I have urgent business to attend to. I shall slip off, if I may, and meet you back here at eleven, after the state banquet, if that suits?'

"Without waiting for a response from the two leaders, the man rose to his feet. Did he really have something else to do, even more urgent than these discussions? I doubt it. He just wanted to make us feel how helpless we were without our phones and sources of information. Howard looked like a ghost. Here he was, in this lavish palace, surrounded by a distinguished crowd with eyes only for him. But he had no means of contact with Washington, his plane had been grounded, and he didn't know what was going on in the rest of the world. In fact, the only information we had was what this man deigned to give us. I suppose he was trying to get us into a state of mind where we would docilely agree to all his demands."

"And what are they, Moro?"

"I've no idea, Alec. Right now, I really don't know. When we met again in the president's office, after the reception and the state banquet, the man simply asked Howard if he would like to address a message to the American people about recent developments. With that in mind, he suggested we meet again on Wednesday morning; by then, the president and his staff would have prepared the text of the address, and he would have dealt with restoring the airwaves. He didn't explicitly say so, but it was understood that the president's words would only be broadcast if they were acceptable to him and his friends. Clearly they were, because Howard was permitted to speak and the cellphone network is up and running again. For the time being, anyway."

"But who are these people? You must have some idea."

"Don't bet on it. I don't know anything. The man just talked about 'us' and 'you.'"

"Is he the leader, do you think?"

"I doubt it. The leader wouldn't have come, and certainly not on his own. But he's certainly more than a mere messenger. In the old days he'd have been called a plenipotentiary. He's very self-assured. He sat there across from two presidents, cool as a cucumber, for all the world like the CEO of a multinational paying a visit to a branch office."

"Do we know anything about him at all?"

"He says he's called Demosthenes."

"Greek?"

"It could just be a nom de guerre. He certainly doesn't look much like any Greeks I know. He has copper-colored skin and speaks English like he's spent his entire life in Massachusetts."

*

I spent the day piecing together what Moro had told me. I tried very hard to recall every detail, since I hadn't taken notes while he was talking.

I know it doesn't matter much, what with everything that's going on, but I must say that the whole way through our conversation I was astonished he was able to talk to me so freely about what was said behind closed doors among the presidential entourage. I didn't want to point this out to him, in order not to break his train of thought, and also because I trust his judgment. As a lawyer and, I assume, as a political advisor, he is usually extremely discreet. But on the other hand, when he's thinking aloud with a friend he can sometimes get so carried away with his analysis that he forgets there might be malicious ears listening in. Eventually it was he who made the point, without my even asking him, breaking off in the middle of a sentence to tell me that the very notion of confidentiality no longer made any sense, "since the only people I need to hide anything from already know everything."

But something else was nagging me. At first it seemed so misplaced and ridiculous that I was embarrassed to admit it to Moro. It was only later in the evening that I convinced myself I absolutely had to have words with him about it.

Let me explain. When my friend described the aforementioned Demosthenes, I immediately thought of Agamemnon. Was it just because both names are ancient Greek, yet neither of them looks Greek? Yes, obviously such a coincidence was bound to intrigue me.

I hesitated initially, for fear of seeming ridiculous. Understandable. That "these people"—I'm using such a vague expression for lack of a better term—deemed it necessary to send an emissary to the most powerful head of state in the world is easy to understand. But why on earth would they have placed a representative on the Chiron archipelago, at the piddling little junction that leads from Port-Atlantique to my tiny island of Antioch? It makes no sense; yes, it's ridiculous. And yet it bothered me, I had to get to the bottom of it. It was past midnight when I picked up the phone to call Moro back.

"I have one more question. What does this Demosthenes look like?"

"He's tall, broad-shouldered, a slightly larger than average head. His coloring is hard to describe, coppery, if you know what I mean. High cheekbones. He looks like an American Indian. Are you already trying to draw him?"

"I will do soon enough. But I asked you to describe him for a different reason. There's someone here."

I told him about Agamemnon. A Greek name and the features of someone from the Comanche tribe. He too seems to have turned up out of nowhere.

Moro said nothing. I imagined him scratching his round head with his stubby fingers, nails bitten down to the quick.

"What you're telling me, Alec, may well have no bearing on our case, but it's possible that it does. In the situation we're in, we can't afford to ignore any leads. If these people have spread out around the world, each of them can teach us something significant. Remember, we're completely in the dark right now. They're there, somewhere, above our heads; they see us, they listen to us, they watch our every move, they tell us this, they allow us that, as they see fit. We can't make a move without their consent. And we know nothing about them, who they are or where they come from or how they operate or what their intentions are. So if you want my advice, don't hesitate. Go and see this Agamemnon. Don't bother with any preamble—time's too short, get straight to the point. Give him the name of Demosthenes, and mine, the president's even. Put all your cards on the table, but make sure he tells you something in return. Anything you can glean will be valuable."

I promised him I'd do it first thing tomorrow, and that I'd get straight back to him.

Patches of Sunlight

"Yes, the light is precious,
but not if I have to pay for it
by losing both my eyes."
Aragon, *The French Diana*

Friday, November 12th

I began the day with the feeling that I owe a moral debt to Moro. He showed me true brotherly love yesterday, taking the time to tell me what's happened, and in such detail. Thanks to his friendship and his trust, I have the illusion that I am at the heart of this global event, while the truth is I live on the fringes of society, far from everything, on my tiny, bare rock.

As a way of demonstrating my gratitude, I promised myself I would check at the earliest opportunity if "my" Agamemnon had any kind of link with "his" Demosthenes.

The earliest opportunity wasn't very early at all. I fell asleep at dawn and slept until around midday. As soon as I got up, I consulted the tide chart. It was high tide, and the Gouay was impassable. Which meant there was no way of getting to the ferryman's house. But I could try and call him.

He answered on the second ring, sounding as upbeat as ever. Given the circumstances, I opted for a more reserved tone.

"I have to talk to you about a few things I've found out. Can we meet?"

"If it's important I can come over in the boat."

"I'd be really grateful."

"I'll put away my tools and be right with you."

Half an hour later I heard the sputtering of an engine. The ferryman made land at the bottom of the garden, tied his mooring rope to a post, and, holding his cap in his hand, walked up to my glazed front door, head tilted slightly to one side. A sign of deference? Of modesty? Was it a little devious, even?

I invited him to sit down and got straight to the point.

"Do you by any chance know a man called Demosthenes?"

Silence. Agamemnon looked me straight in the eye. He seemed to be weighing up his options. After a moment he said, "It's a name from where I come from."

An ambiguous response. An ambiguous smile. I forced myself to look as assured as I could. But my throat was tight. To give myself the illusion of composure, I picked up a cigarillo from the coffee table and lit it.

"I'm talking about a man who turned up on Tuesday in Santiago, in Chile, with a message for the president of the United States."

Again the ferryman fixed his gaze on me. He continued to appear undecided. Then a gleam of determination lit up his face.

"I understood that," he said. "He's definitely from where I come from."

I was slightly disconcerted. I'd been expecting an evasive response, followed by a lengthy pursuit through a winding labyrinth. It was almost as if his admission had come too soon. The ball was now in my court, and I couldn't let it roll to a stop. "As it happens, a friend from my student days is in the president's entourage. I managed to speak to him yesterday. He told me his version of what's happened."

And then I told the ferryman in a reasonable amount of detail what Moro had shared with me:

the operation that had been planned against Sardarov's stronghold; Sardarov's threats; Milton's order to strike; the sudden communications blackout; and finally how this Demosthenes had showed up at La Moneda. The ferryman listened attentively, without interrupting or asking any questions. When I stopped, he spoke with his characteristic good humor.

"Didn't I tell you the world had avoided a disaster and it was too soon for lamentations?"

I responded with a polite smile, but his wisecrack didn't allay my disquiet. I pressed him: "Was there anything in what I just told you that you didn't already know?"

He hesitated. As if he were trying to find the right way to formulate his response.

"What you just told me confirms and adds to what I already knew."

I said nothing, simply looked at him meaningfully to make it clear I was waiting for him to continue. Agamemnon began to repeat what I'd just told him, adding his own observations. "Everything points to two things: Marshal Sardarov decided to attack multiple cities around the world with his nuclear warheads. And to prevent him the American president ordered a massive aerial bombardment of the Caucasian military bases. A two-pronged escalation ..."

He left his sentence unfinished. I waited. He didn't say anything else. I pressed him.

"This two-pronged escalation, as you call it, had to be averted, is that right?"

"Yes, clearly."

"And you intervened to avert it, is that right?"

"Yes, that's right."

"But that means you had to have the means to prevent it."

He nodded. I repeated, patiently, "To paralyze the belligerents, you had to have the ability to immediately block all means of communication, in order to prevent Sardarov from transmitting orders to his army, and Milton from communicating with the Pentagon."

He nodded again.

"So you do have those means?"

"You clearly believe we do," he said, inclining his head slightly to one side, as though the admission of the formidable power of his people had to be accompanied by a gesture of humility.

In the course of this exchange my voice had been growing gradually louder. Now I had to restrain myself to keep from yelling "*Who are you?*"

Perhaps it would have been better had I started with that question. Hadn't he thrown me a line when he'd confessed that the man named Demosthenes was one of them? My question could hardly have come as a surprise, and he was clearly prepared for it. Even so, he seemed embarrassed and, like his compatriot when Milton had asked him the same question, he played for time.

"It's hard for me to talk to you today as frankly as I'd like. This is a delicate moment, and I'm afraid there's no way I can say anything here, now, on the island, even as a friend, which could compromise any ongoing negotiations. Just know that my people are not in the pay of any nation or any power, and that they have only one objective: to avert global catastrophe. They'll be more than eager to return to their role as spectators as soon as the danger has passed."

"And you'll go back to being the Antioch ferryman."

"I've never stopped."

An insincere smile, on both sides. A few seconds of silence. Then, with a touch of exasperation, I said:

"You really have nothing else to tell me?"

Agamemnon was about to answer when there was a knock on the door. Though a quite banal occurrence anywhere else, on the island it was incongruous, and at this stage in our conversation, somewhat ill-timed. But I had to open it. It was Ève—it was bound to be, I should say, given that no one could cross the Gouay at high tide, and she was the island's only other inhabitant. Still, it was the very first time she had paid me a visit. It was early afternoon, so it practically constituted a morning visit, in view of her lifestyle.

Seeing I wasn't alone, she said a little awkwardly that she would come back later. I politely assured her that she wasn't disturbing us.

To be honest, I wasn't sure if I was annoyed or relieved to see her. On the one hand, I assumed that Agamemnon wouldn't be prepared to reveal anything more about himself in front of a third person; on the other, I was feeling uncomfortable just the two of us and wasn't sorry to see my neighbor turn up.

As for the ferryman, he looked positively delighted by the intrusion. I even had the impression he'd been hoping for it. He immediately became much more talkative, addressing himself directly to Ève.

"I came to see you once, Madame Saint-Gilles, and quoted a passage from your excellent novel. You won't remember the exact words, but I shall never forget them."

I glanced over to my neighbor as he was speaking. She didn't look remotely flattered; she seemed absent, or deaf. I'd already noticed that she grew exaggeratedly irritated whenever I referred to her novel. She was one of those writers who, having only published one successful work, spends the rest of their life trying to get away from it, ending up loathing it as if it were the ceiling of their prison cell. My neighbor was, in this respect, a living caricature. As soon as the ferryman mentioned her book she turned away. She drew a large exhibition catalog at random from the bookshelf and began ostentatiously leafing through it, pretending to be completely absorbed and unable to hear what was being said. But Agamemnon pressed on, quite unperturbed.

"You wrote this: *On the paths of life we find ourselves continuously coming up against the burdensome corpses of our history. But what if one day humanity, tired of struggling with its past, were to encounter its future— would it be able to recognize it? And would it be able to recognize itself in this future, and lay its hands flat on its powerful and warm body?* Well, Madame, if that was a premonition, it's been verified, and if it was a wish, it's been granted."

I threw a glance at Agamemnon to excuse my visitor's rudeness, when Ève literally dropped the catalog on the floor. She turned towards the ferryman, her face transformed, and walked over to him, beaming as if she were in the presence of a miraculous apparition. I thought for a moment she was going to throw herself into his arms or at his feet. But she stopped a few feet away, looked him straight in the eye, and asked, "Who are you?"

The question, the only one. The one that the incidents of the last few days have compelled everyone on earth to wonder. The one that Howard Milton had asked Demosthenes and I, Agamemnon, without either of us getting an answer. But now the ferryman looked embarrassed. He asked me if he could have one of my cigarillos, lit a match, and let the flame burn for a moment before bringing it to the tip. I thought I saw his fingers trembling. And I understood in a flash why he had been sent to this unlikely place in this guise. Because of Ève, of course! To keep an eye on her. Evidently these men felt affection for her, veneration even.

I was no longer at all sorry for my neighbor's intrusion. Thanks to her, embarrassment had swapped sides. Or at least it was shared more equally between us now.

"Where do you want me to start?" said Agamemnon. And this time, I think, his reticence wasn't faked.

"With your name," Ève suggested firmly. "What is the meaning of this reference to Ancient Greece?"

"Yes, that's the right approach, let's start there. It is not by chance that we all took Greek names. We have aligned ourselves with its civilization, with particular admiration for what some historians call the 'Athenian miracle,' that extraordinary moment when the human spirit blossomed in multiple disciplines, all at the same time—when theater, philosophy, medicine, history, sculpture, architecture, and democracy were, if you like, 'invented.' All by a small number of men in the space of a few decades. A creative profusion that has never seen any equivalent, neither in the centuries before nor in those that followed. Which came out of nowhere and was stamped out just as suddenly. It took another two millennia for the world to experience a semblance of a rebirth.

"What would have happened if humanity, instead of sinking into the long Middle Ages, had continued to develop as in the blessed era of the Greek miracle? How would the arts, sciences, and philosophy have evolved? How might the human intellect have soared if it had continued to flourish at that pace in so many different fields? These are all questions, Madame, that you yourself ask so lucidly in your novel. Just as you express nostalgia for the unparalleled era that gave us Socrates, Plato, Euripides, Herodotus, Hippocrates, Phidias, Aristotle, and so many others.

"Now, let's forget the history books for a moment. Lend your ears to the beautiful story my parents used to tell me about what my distant ancestors are supposed to have experienced, if not dreamed or imagined.

"The moment the miracle's flame began to stutter, a few beings, braver than the rest, decided they had to act. How many were they? A handful. They knew their civilization was going to founder, and that they had to preserve its ideals at any cost. So off they went. They set sail from Attica, Boeotia, Thessaly, the Peloponnese, and according to legend all they took with them was what they had in their heads. And that is how my forebears' adventure began.

"At the time, exile was experienced as punishment, an amputation, almost like suicide. Which explains, no doubt, why these men named themselves after an individual who had died several decades earlier by throwing himself into the crater of a volcano."

"Empedocles of Agrigento," said Ève solemnly.

"The very same. My ancestors were known as 'the friends of Empedocles.' And that's what we have always called ourselves."

I was glad to find this out, if for no other reason than that it meant I could stop using vague and slightly distasteful terms like "those people" to describe them.

"What about the others?" Ève asked. "Other human beings, what do you call them?"

"We have various names for them, Madame. Sometimes we just say, 'the others,' or even 'them.' Or 'the people,' or 'the multitude,' or even—"

"The multitude! The multitude!" Ève repeated in a lilting voice, as if to make it clear that she'd made her choice.

The ferryman stopped listing names.

"And what do you call your country, Agam?" I asked.

"We just say 'Empedocles' … But don't bother trying to find it on a map."

He smiled, and I understood that that was all he was prepared to say. So I returned to the previous topic.

"Your ancestors, their exodus from Greece, is it a myth, or a true story?"

"The story is true, because we believe it is," he said with a chuckle. "In any case, my parents always told me it was the true story of where we came from, which meant that my whole life I knew who I was, where I came from, where I had to head for, and the purpose of my existence."

He was trying to sound persuasive, but his words remained opaque.

"So how did these exiles from Ancient Greece manage to acquire such power?" Ève asked.

"That is indeed the primordial question that current events are likely to elicit," said Agamemnon. "I promise to give you an answer soon. But not yet. Things are too delicate for me to be able to talk to you as openly as I'd like right now. All being well, in a few days I'll be able to satisfy your curiosity."

As he reached the end of the sentence his cell-phone rang. He stood up, nodded an apology, and walked out the room. He came back in only to say, "Sorry, I must go. We'll talk more later."

He bowed to my neighbor, laid an old-fashioned kiss on her hand, and disappeared, leaving us both awash in his strange words, and quite unsatisfied.

*

I turned to Ève, hoping for some comment from her that would chime with the thoughts churning in my mind. But the expression in her eyes was like the reflection of a church candle. Out of respect for her reverie, a rapture that was palpable and profound, I said nothing, or at least not out loud; in my mind I was going over every sentence I'd just heard. I wanted to be sure to remember it all, so I'd be able to reproduce it later without error.

Agamemnon has, in plain language, delivered what can only be called a revelation. Yes, a revelation, after which nothing will ever be the same again. Humanity, the Earth, History, right down to our everyday lives.

"I need to walk by the sea," said my neighbor suddenly. "Will you come?"

We wandered towards the beach known as the Lilac Sands, after the purplish seaweed that's deposited there at high tide. It slopes very gently there, and we had to go quite a long way out to reach the ocean. Ève's expression was that of a sleepwalker, silent and contemplative, but her step was brisk and sometimes she even skipped. She was in the kind of trance that ordinary mortals attain by inhaling quite different substances to sea air.

When we reached the water's edge she continued walking into the water at the same pace. I grabbed her arm to pull her back. She didn't struggle, she wasn't suicidal; she was euphoric, almost triumphant. But the ocean doesn't care what mood you're in, it would have swallowed her up anyway. Every beach on the Chiron Islands has its chaplet of the reckless and the presumptuous, and the old salts from La Cap-Hornière never get bored of listing their names and circumstances.

Holding on to her with both hands, I led her back to the bracken and wild blackberry-lined path. She began pirouetting like a little girl in her flowered dress, stumbling now and again. I held her firmly by the hand, refusing to let go. Not that she was trying to get away; her fingers gripped mine and each time she leaned her head against my shoulder her hair blew into my eyes.

When I got her home she invited me in, and began turning on all the lights in the house.

"Sit down for a bit, we're not going to let an evening like this just fizzle out, are we? I'll go get the champagne."

Good grief, to celebrate what? What I'd found out today had made me feel introspective, not festive. I felt like I needed calmly to mull over my future, all our futures, our place in the world.

It seems clear that a new era has begun, though I know nothing about it. It's as if I've been forcibly deported to a continent that I didn't even know existed. What will I find there? I haven't the slightest idea. And I certainly can't tell yet if it's something to welcome or regret.

At the same time, I wasn't unmoved by my neighbor's euphoria. I watched her with a kind of brotherly affection. I had no desire to knock the wind out of her sails—it was so unusual for her to be happy. I lifted my glass. After all, we did have at least one reason to celebrate. With all the enthusiasm I could muster, I proclaimed, "To our survival! We could have died this evening, the two of us and millions of others, if this stupid conflict had blown up."

Ève raised her brimming glass but didn't take it to her lips. If I'd imagined this would be a way of bonding with her, it hadn't worked. She lowered the glass, her expression clouded, and she turned to stare into the fire at the last of the glowing embers. When she raised the glass again it wasn't towards me, but over her head, as though she were making a toast to herself alone.

"I have something else to toast. I'm not drinking because men have been saved, or because they've had another close call, despite their madness. I'm drinking and rejoicing because humankind has finally discovered its masters. I'm drinking to the friends of Empedocles! Now human arrogance has been smashed to the ground."

She put her feet up on the coffee table, held her glass to her lips like a microphone and declared, as though stirring up an imaginary crowd, "We thought we were the kings of the universe, the apex of creation—the Everest of creation!—with our glorious past, our prodigious scholarship, our venerable religions ..." She emptied her glass in a single swallow and continued, "Even when we acknowledged that our civilizations were mortal, we still managed to be pompous and arrogant. We thought we'd reached the end of History. It turns out we hadn't even left prehistory behind."

She held her glass out towards me to refill it. I drank with her, without saying a word.

"We might be less angry if the others were merely stronger. But they're actually better! Better in every way. Freer, purer, more honest."

What did she know about them?

"And all our beliefs, our traditions, our knowledge? I shouldn't think they give two hoots about them, just like we secretly laugh at the rites of other cultures."

Now I couldn't help but speak. "My dear Ève, what do you know about all this?"

She looked at me in horrified surprise, as if I were the last person in the world to get it, to understand. And she repeated in her own words the legend told to us by the ferryman.

"Long ago, humanity was split in two. Some people departed, like emigrants going to establish a new city. The others stayed. Since then, there have been two parallel groups of humankind. One lives in the light but carries shadow. The other lives in the shadows but carries light. Each one has continued at its own pace along its own path."

The same legend, the same revelation, revisited, interpreted, and embellished by my neighbor the novelist. But the way Ève told it, it was if she were talking about real events, recorded since time immemorial in books that I am apparently the only person in the world never to have read.

Perhaps she's right. For my part, I'm skeptical. Who makes up that other branch of humankind? Where do they live? Where are their houses, their factories, their laboratories? How come we never suspected their existence until the beginning of the third millennium? I didn't buy what she was saying, but with no arguments to contradict her I stayed silent. My neighbor was in full flow. "The friends of Empedocles have kept on walking straight ahead, not letting themselves get caught up in our squabbles or distracted by our stupid beliefs. And now they're far ahead of us in all fields of knowledge, and in the art of happiness as well. I want to drink to them. To our rediscovered brothers!"

Wearily, I joined in her toast. We got through one bottle, then two more, though I drank no more than a quarter of each. I was surprised that someone so resolutely bleak in outlook had stashed away such a lot of champagne.

"Let's drink to Empedocles!"

I wasn't displeased to see her so jovial, so exuberant. I toasted everything she proposed, while my thoughts sped in thirty different directions. Sometimes Ève's words seduced me; not only did I find myself agreeing, but I'd have happily said the same things myself—after all, the reason I'd chosen to withdraw to my island was because of my frustration at the state of the world. But then I'd change my mind again: supposing Agamemnon and Demosthenes's compatriots were really what they appeared to be—omnipotent, perfect, a distinctly superior version of humankind—what would become of us, me and my fellow ordinary humans? Quarrelsome natives, cloistered in our reserves, surrounded by barbed wire? An inferior species, Creation's last draft, for archaeologists and paleontologists and experts in the exotic to study in the future? What would become of our science, our languages, our religions, our legends, our heroes, all the things we're so proud of and whose memory sustains us? How would we carry on living when we were no longer proud of who we were? We have our flaws, I told myself, we can be utterly insufferable, criminal, barbarous. But that's who we are!

To go back to my comparison from the other day: if I'd been an Aztec artist, and one of my friends had been close to Moctezuma, would I have rejoiced at the advance of the Spanish, how efficient their weapons were, the military acumen of the conquistadors?

I said nothing of all this to Ève. She was too excited to listen and, by the end of the evening, too drunk. And the fact is that over so many years of living alone I've gotten out of the habit of arguing, lost all interest in it. I debate things in my head, and if ever I raise my voice in jubilation or rebellion, it's in my cartoons.

*

While I was at my neighbor's house I took a moment to slip away to the bathroom and send a message to Moro asking him to get in touch as soon as possible, so I could tell him what I'd found out. He didn't call me back until around midnight my time: he'd spent all day in the air.

"Our magnanimous guardians let us leave Santiago and return to Washington," he told me with a hollow laugh. Despite the humiliating circumstances, he was relieved. "Howard couldn't bear being out of the country anymore. I don't know if you noticed how he carefully omitted to mention in his address on Wednesday that he was speaking from Chile; he feared this would be extremely disconcerting to the American people. Add to that the fact that his health requires a number of daily medications that can only be properly dispensed at his living quarters at the White House."

"You mean they wouldn't let you go until now?"

"Not explicitly. But you understand we couldn't take off if there was any risk of losing contact with air traffic control. When we asked Demosthenes yesterday if he could guarantee that Air Force One wouldn't encounter any difficulties, he simply offered to join us on the flight, which was the best possible guarantee."

"So he took the plane with you?"

"Yes. I'll tell you about it. But you go first. Tell me what you've found out."

I recounted my conversation with the ferryman, trying not to omit any details. Moro let me finish without saying a word, but I sensed from the tenor of his breathing that he was impressed. When I'd finished he rewarded me with a hearty and very American "Wow!"

"Almost everything you've just told me, Alec, is new to me. We discussed strategy, nuclear warfare, and disarmament with Demosthenes. None of us asked him where he was from, and he didn't say. I did hear him once mention the name Empedocles. We were on the airplane. I managed to grab five minutes next to him before we took off. I don't need to tell you that the seat was coveted by a good number of people. To engage him in conversation, partly to be polite and partly to test his reaction, I said to him that once this diplomatic crisis was over I'd very much like to visit his homeland. He smiled and said, 'Why not? Do you like very long journeys?' I said, 'Yes, they don't worry me.' 'And very short journeys?' I think he was teasing me a little, but I said, 'I don't hate them.' 'Well then, you'd be most welcome in the country of Empedocles!' I said, 'Sicily, you mean?' He laughed. 'Our territory is in Sicily in the same way that I am Greek.' He shook my hand.

Cynthia, the first lady, was standing in the corridor alongside us, clearly impatient. I stood up, and she sat down in my place."

As usual, Moro is absorbing it all with good humor and grace. But there is no doubt he is unnerved.

*

At the end of this long day, I've been rereading what I've written so far, all the strange things I've recorded, and I don't know what to think. I've been spun a good yarn—too good to be true. It might be just a myth, but in my bemused frame of mind it's tempting to believe it, even if it means silencing the voice of reason within me.

It seems then there is a twofold human race. The world as a theater, with two plays being performed simultaneously, one visible, the other underground; one characterized by lack of awareness—our history—and the other the custodian of wisdom and salvation, but also, for us, the promise of humiliation. Was I supposed to follow my neighbor's example and celebrate this with champagne? Wouldn't it be more appropriate to be in mourning?

For the time being I reserve my opinion.

It often rains through the night on Antioch, then in the morning the empty clouds part and the light returns. Such is the generosity of the Atlantic skies.

It didn't begin raining until late last night and the rain trespassed into the early morning. Towards eleven the sun came out; it wasn't warm, but the light was dazzling on the limewashed walls and made the dewdrops and puddles glisten.

I was woken by the phone. It was my goddaughter Adrienne responding to my message, apologizing for not having gotten back to me sooner. She's spent the last three days and nights of chaos at the hospital. Eight people have died in her sector since Tuesday because the communication blackout meant medical personnel couldn't reach people in time. Apparently her partner Charles, also an emergency physician, is incandescent with rage. She, on the other hand, is taking it all philosophically. "If what happened means we avoided a nuclear nightmare," she told me, "at least those unfortunate souls won't have died in vain."

After we'd spoken I hung up and jumped out of bed, pulled on a pair of jeans, prepared a thermos of coffee, and sat down at my drawing table. For four days I haven't so much as drawn a single line, and I don't want to settle into indolence. It's not as if time has stopped; it's simply on hold. Sooner or later the newspapers will start publishing again, on paper and online, and I'll have to start supplying them with cartoon strips as before. I opened my sketchbook at the first blank page and picked up my stout drawing pencil. That's how I get my flashes of inspiration. Its silvery casing attracts them like a lightning conductor.

Suddenly there was silence. It was already quiet, but there are different levels, densities. I couldn't tell you what was different about this silence. I pressed the on button of the radio: again that rhythmic whistling.

Damn! It had started again!

Without stopping to think, I ran to the garage, got on my bike, and began cycling furiously towards the Gouay. I had to see the ferryman, convey my anger, and most importantly get him to tell me why we were being punished like this again.

God, it's exhilarating, cycling like that over the ocean. It's exhilarating, and also calming. The color; the smell of seaweed; the sheer scale of it, so close! The symphony of the lapping waves. All the worries of the world are submerged in it, get broken into pieces, and drown. I had to hold tight to my anger to keep from losing it along the way.

Agamemnon wasn't home, and his dinghy wasn't where it's usually tied up. I rang the bell, knocked, turned the door handle. It wasn't locked. I pushed it open and went in, calling, "Agam!" One thing led to another and I found myself, without having planned to, inspecting shelves, cupboards, drawers, boxes, searching under tables, rummaging beneath the bed and the wardrobe. What was I after? An object of some kind—a device, a picture, a book, a map, a little statue—bearing a sign of the country of Empedocles. I've never done anything like that before in my life. But it's also true that I've never felt such a sense of dread either.

I found nothing at the ferryman's house. Nothing that gave away his "homeland." Even his two nautical radios, with their distinctly futuristic appearance, had both been made by "us," if I could put it that way. I checked—one was made in Denmark, one in South Korea.

I decided to take a stroll around Port-Atlantique. Nothing to report there either. La Cap-Hornière was as crowded as usual. All the regulars were there—Gautier, old Antonin, and the others. A bit less raucous than usual, lots of low murmuring. I harvested plenty of predictable questions. No answers at all.

Rumors were circulating in hushed tones. I won't bother to recount them here. What's the point? I'll be getting verifiable information soon enough. Though perhaps I ought to mention the scruffy young man, cigarette dangling from his lip, who sometimes shakes my hand and addresses me with casual familiarity but whose name I don't know, who came over to ask me if I didn't agree with him that "our ferryman" seemed like a shifty kind of guy. Around us, ears pricked up. I answered carefully that Agamemnon had always seemed to me to be honest and obliging. That was all I said. The young man drifted away. The others didn't say a word.

The atmosphere was becoming oppressive. I hurriedly took my leave.

*

Towards the end of the afternoon, I went over to my neighbor's house. She, like me, thinks that somewhere in the world something bad has happened again today. But she has no more idea than I what that might be. It doesn't seem to worry her. She's still smiling like an avenging angel, or a prisoner freed before the end of his sentence.

She insisted I stay for dinner, assuring me that she wasn't going to cook, the meal would be very simple. And indeed, she simply opened a jar of preserved tuna, a specialty of the islands, and a bottle of Entre-Deux-Mers. Just as we were sitting down to eat, she announced, standing to attention like a little girl pretending to be a palace guard, "A sailor's supper by candlelight!"

When scarcity becomes privilege ...

It was the first time I've sat down to eat at Ève's table, but not the first meal I've shared with her. Whenever I can't be bothered to cook—a fairly common occurrence—I phone the only delicatessen on the islands, La Dorade Coryphène, which always has seven or eight different dishes on offer. Its name is pretentious, but I don't hold that against the owners, because everything they prepare is so tasty and fresh. So much so that I can never choose. "Sea bass or seven-hour lamb with white beans?" the chef's wife will murmur in an alluring voice. Just as I'm about to choose she adds: "Or what about *gambas à la sauce armoricaine*?" To conquer my indecision I'll ask, "What's my neighbor having?" Nine times out of ten I end up ordering the same as her. At low tide the same driver delivers both our meals, which we each sit down to eat at our own table.

Put like this, my life must sound very dull. But for someone who worships silence and tranquility, to the point of having chosen to live and draw on an almost deserted island, there is nothing sad about this routine. I have no regrets, no bitterness.

After all, what does a man really need? If he has good health and a decent internet connection, everything else is trivial. I wouldn't go so far as to say, in the words of the existentialist philosopher, that hell is other people. But they're not paradise either.

That said, I was actually very happy to spend the evening in Ève's company. Even if the menu wasn't on a par with what our caterer usually treats us to.

Our conversation over dinner wasn't limited to current events. I told Ève all about my parents, my ancestry, what had led me to leave Montreal to come and live on Antioch. She, in turn, told me about her family, and what had led her too to come and settle here. Her mother was a half-Irish, half-Jamaican singer who'd had her fifteen minutes of fame, but also suffered lengthy periods of depression and hospitalization. Her father was a commercial pilot from Toulouse. He travelled a great deal and probably had a mistress in every port. Ève had spent her childhood waiting for him; as she said this she sighed deeply, as though it continued to upset her thirty years later.

Every time he returned from Europe to America, Captain Saint-Gilles used to fly over our island, and he always talked with longing of this "pink pebble linked to the coast by a silver thread." He promised himself he would move here one day, a dream he never fulfilled but that he bequeathed to his daughter. A little like what my father had done for me. As a result of this "transmission of dreams" our respective journeys, despite their differences, bear a certain similarity.

My neighbor talked this evening with a calm she hadn't felt in years. The sudden appearance of the friends of Empedocles has reconciled her with her past and with what is still her first and only novel—which she'd long since turned against but is now beginning to appreciate again, having heard it quoted with such reverence from the lips of Agamemnon.

Actually, I'm beginning to realize with every passing day how Ève's take on the ongoing situation is having an effect on my own reactions, making me more conciliatory, more understanding of our new overseers. Even though I don't agree with everything she says, even though I might correct her, criticize her, and tease her, her rediscovered sense of joy is making me less suspicious of "them" than I would have been if left to my own devices. Without her as my guide, how would I have been able to raise my glass so joyfully to the obliteration of our history and the death of our civilization?

*

I dozed off a little earlier, and now I've woken up and lit a candle so I can continue writing this journal. There's one subject I've chosen to pass over, but now

I feel compelled to bring it up. This evening I had the urgent desire to spend the night with Ève, and I have the feeling the same idea occurred to her; all evening she kept casting glances at me, making gestures, dropping hints.

There's no doubt about it, since the beginning of what we're living through, ever since my first evening visit to her dark, cold house, every day I've been feeling a little closer to her. My change in attitude is obvious in this diary, and the reality of my feelings goes even deeper. I've occasionally described my neighbor in slightly unflattering, even quite unkind terms, but now I see her very differently. I'm not going to go back and censor my words, cross out the description of her "prematurely faded looks" and the other regrettable things I've written about her. That would be petty falsification. The only honest way to correct my failure to appreciate her is to describe how as of today I simply no longer think of my neighbor in the same way as I did before. I don't know if her wrinkles have been smoothed away, but I don't see them now, they don't matter anymore. Agamemnon's revelations have literally transfigured Ève Saint-Gilles and completely changed how I feel towards her. Even if I don't share her ideas, I feel genuine affection for her, tenderness even. And this evening I wanted to hold her tightly in my arms.

What stopped me? A nagging inner voice I couldn't silence: if I let the only other inhabitant of the island into my life, my remarkably peaceful existence will come to an end. If things were ever to go wrong between us, life on Antioch would become hellish and one of us would have to leave—me, no doubt. Am I ready to take such a risk?

I'm aware that confessing to this dilemma so candidly must make me sound cold and calculating, impervious to what other people like to call the enchantment of love. I'm not really. But it is true that I am prepared for any amount of sacrifice and suffering to preserve this blessed territory, my solitude.

Sunday, November 14th

Yesterday I had so little information about what was going on around the world that I was reduced to recording in this notebook every tiny detail, down to the menu for our candlelit dinner and my old bachelor qualms. Today I have received news, albeit in dribs and drabs. The blackouts are sporadic and unpredictable. The radio will work for fifteen minutes, then stop for an hour, come back, then stop again. The telephone and internet are worse: it's like the network only functions every other minute—which would drive even the most level-headed person crazy.

Is this a subtle form of torture that our so-called guardians have come up with as a way of punishing us? I think it's probably more a show of force intended to impress, intimidate, and subdue us. They want to make it clear that they can modify their sanctions as and when they wish. As if they're sitting in front of a vast planisphere, entertaining themselves by turning the lights off here, switching them on over there; preventing conversations here, permitting them over there. In fact—why deny it?—I'm impressed. But most of all I feel humiliated, and my heart is filled with an unfamiliar bitterness.

In this unsettling context, I really don't know what to make of the optimistic—exaggeratedly so—address by President Milton today, his second since the start of the crisis. His wavering voice was introduced by a brief announcement specifying that this time he was speaking "live from the White House."

My fellow Americans,

Last Wednesday I spoke to you about the situation we find ourselves in. Since then, we have been talking with representatives of the intervening power. Our discussions have not always been easy, but we have gotten through this challenge with an attitude that combines honesty, dignity, and mutual respect. And, for the moment, the skies appear to be less stormy.

In the course of several days of negotiation we have discussed at length the worrying situation resulting from the build-up of nuclear weapons and radioactive fissile substances. As these cannot at this time be efficiently neutralized, our experts estimate that they will need to be stored, in an unstable state, for a period that is to all intents and purposes indefinite. In various places around the United States, highly dangerous materials have been amassed in substantial quantities, and I frequently wonder what would happen if wicked people—members of an extremist group, for example, or madmen, or people driven by greed—were to detonate a deadly device at one of these storage sites. In other places around the world, notably in the former Soviet Union, radioactive weapons and substances remain stockpiled in alarming conditions, and dangerous materials have fallen into the hands of some notoriously irresponsible individuals.

During our discussions with the representatives of the intervening power, we have come to the conclusion that they bear us no ill will; indeed, on the contrary, they are acting with great consideration for our country, for the principles of our Constitution, and for our way of life, and they acknowledge our prominent position among the nations. We also believe that they are in possession of a peaceable technology enabling them to effectively treat radioactive substances, rendering them harmless both for humans and for our planet.

My fellow Americans,

The development of nuclear weapons was a necessary evil at a certain period in our history. We always knew it was a dangerous form of energy and could potentially be used for malign purposes, but we had to bring the Second World War to an end, after which we were faced with a new threat, that of Communism. Today, the biggest threat to our civilization is the proliferation of nuclear weapons and the risk of them falling into the hands of criminals, as happened recently. The beast has been unleashed, it is untamable, and it is of the utmost urgency that we lead it carefully back into its cage and lock it up forever.

The friends whom providence has brought to us promise to deal with this in the coming days. With the agreement of the US government, and in strict accordance with our institutions, they will undertake a total clean-up operation, aimed at ridding the planet of every device, every instrument, and all materials that pose a threat to the survival of the human race.

I would like solemnly to request that all members of our armed forces, in particular those posted at sensitive installations, my fellow Americans, and every man and woman of goodwill the world over, do all that is necessary to enable our friends to carry out the delicate operation that we have agreed upon with them.

In a few days' time we will have gotten through this challenging period and we will, I hope, find ourselves living in a safer, more peaceful and stable world and a healthier environment.

I have faith, and I am asking you to have faith. Faith in our great nation, and faith in our ability to achieve things

as marvelous as those achieved by our forebears. Faith in
our allies. Faith in the future.

God bless you!

God bless the United States of America!

I listened to Milton's address, and taped it so I'd be able to listen to it again. He appeared, like last time, to be trying to sound reassuring, but what he was implying was not very reassuring at all. It was hard not to hear in his words an admission of powerlessness. Not only of his nation, but of all of us who find ourselves from one day to the next the vassals of a new overlord. I was dying to hear what Moro made of it. I tried calling him, to no avail. My cellphone was working, but his gave no sign of life.

If I had to offer my impressions in my usual manner, in other words by the pen of my alter ego, Alec Zander, I would do so in three linked drawings. In the first, I would draw the US president in close-up, his emaciated face behind an old-fashioned microphone; in the second, wider image, I'd show his arms connected to a drip; in the third, wider still, I'd show a small, very sick man surrounded by a group of fierce soldiers pointing their weapons at him. Because it was fairly obvious that Milton had spoken, and was pretending to be optimistic, under duress.

Don't think I'm criticizing Moro's friend. I sympathize with him, and in a sense I admire him too.

It takes courage and wisdom to disguise a national and civilizational catastrophe as hope.

This evening, after I had conscientiously completed my chronicler's and diarist's assignments and sketched out in pencil the cartoons described above, I walked over to Ève's house to discuss the president's latest address. I didn't find her. Her front door was locked and the house was dark. There was a light on outside, as if to light the way home. I rang the bell and tried the handle without success. So I walked to the Lilac Sands, hoping to find her at the place where two days ago we'd laughed together. There was no one there.

The moon was veiled in wispy clouds; it looked full, or nearly full, and cast a white light over the ground and the surface of the ocean. I wandered along the shore, thinking about Ève and me, the things that connect and separate us. About the time we've spent together and our mutual reticence. About my faintly dishonorable dilemmas and confused emotions.

What I do know is that I want to see her all the time, I want to listen to her and to share the myriad thoughts going through my mind. Even when I'm alone, I find myself speaking to her in my head, I picture her jumping up, getting impassioned, frowning. I was sad to have missed her this evening. And I would undoubtedly suffer if I were to stop seeing her. At the same time, after all these years I can't pretend I haven't turned into a complete loner. It's true of my neighbor too. And that means I can't imagine us in a long-term relationship, or being in anything that resembles love.

I'm not proud of these sentiments, of what these long years have made me. Am I still capable of falling in love? Of commitment? Of getting close to someone, unreservedly, holding my breath, without it immediately turning into the penultimate theme of my latest cartoon?

To be honest, the answer is no. No, I'm no longer capable of loving. And sadder still, I'm not even sad about it. Where my heart should be there's a prickly hedgehog instead. Ève is not to blame.

*

Speaking of her, again, I must point out that after having searched for her in vain at her home and then at the beach, I spent the rest of the evening trying to locate my copy of her novel, also in vain.

I've mentioned it already, *The Future Doesn't Live Here Anymore*, which to my great shame I've never read. The day I found out, five or six years ago, that the novelist was planning to move to my island, I rushed to order it. I vowed to read it immediately to get to know my future neighbor. But after my first attempt at a visit, when she was so rude, my irritation was such that I never opened the book. I didn't even bother taking it out of its packaging. I don't know which pile it's buried under. It must be somewhere in my disordered library. I'm going to have to comb through all the shelves, piles, and boxes, even those in the attic.

Back then I wanted nothing to do with the book or its author. I was punishing it, as I'd have liked to punish her for her discourtesy. Now that I feel quite differently towards its begetter, I shall have to change my opinion about her progeny as well.

That said, the reason it's time for me to read Ève's

book is not so much because our relationship has changed. Far more importantly it's because her book has been read and admired by the friends of Empedocles who, if the ferryman is to be believed, consider it a prophetic and visionary work. As soon as our guardians' appreciation becomes widely known, the whole world is going to rush to this book to find the key, to look for answers and reasons to hope. Even more so if it indeed contains, as I understand it does, an introduction to a parallel world to ours— an encounter with which, in a way, is an encounter with our future.

I'll have to keep looking for it tomorrow, in daylight, and eventually I'm bound to lay my hands on it.

Monday, November 15th

Since this morning it's been incredibly stormy, and also in a way all very calm. The elements have been unleashed, while our devices have gone quiet. The airwaves appear to have been completely muzzled.

Nothing about any of this is surprising. Not the bad weather, which is entirely normal for this time of year, nor the blackout, which I assume, logically, must be total, if the clean-up operation that Milton talked about is now underway, with delicate operations at numerous sites so that the nuclear beast can be returned to its cage.

I understand why we're being left in the dark about what's happening. But it doesn't stop me cursing every time I turn on the radio to hear the same jingle indicating that broadcasting has been interrupted, or yet another repeat of the president's call for all citizens, civilian and military, to support the task of the intervening power.

Thank God for Ève! I tried in vain to find her yesterday, and now she's back. She didn't tell me where she was, and I managed not to ask. Perhaps she was quite simply at home, shut away, not wanting to see anyone. Anyway, her mood hasn't changed at all since that moment of grace I wrote about three days ago when, after what the ferryman told us, she dropped the book she'd been leafing through and was suddenly transformed. The gleam that lit up her eyes then is still there. I never want it to be extinguished, even if I don't share her illusions.

When I went to visit her this evening, she repeated

her boundless faith in the friends of Empedocles. My own instinct counsels circumspection. That doesn't mean I reject her opinion. Indeed, a part of me would like to believe she's right.

I've written before in these pages that Ève's outlook is the opposite of mine: she withdrew from the world because she loathed other people, whereas I did so because I wanted to get a better perspective. But this distinction no longer seems very pertinent. The judgement we both bring to bear on the world is similar, even if we each express it in our own way, according to our differing points of view.

The difference between us lies elsewhere. Ève, who as a half-Jamaican woman feels in her very bones the injustices suffered for millennia by her sisters, deems herself bound by no loyalty towards the men who until just a few days ago dominated the planet; she considers that she owes them nothing, and that she has the absolute right to prefer the friends of Empedocles.

Her attitude doesn't offend me, but I can't adopt it. I could never rail as she does against other human beings. As critical as I am of them, I am also aware that I am not only in their midst, but I am one of them; their history is mine. Their faults shame me, their achievements make me proud, and their failures sadden me. I cannot rejoice to see them brought down. Yet what's been happening since this all began is exactly that.

Do my fellow humans deserve this humiliation? Yes, undoubtedly—on this point I'm tempted to agree with Ève. The difference between us is that she is delighted while I am dismayed.

But once again this evening we drank champagne together and raised our glasses: she to bless Empedocles's followers for the chaos they have set in motion; me to toast in a dignified manner the memory of the miracle of Ancient Greece, hoping that it will light our way without blinding us.

This difference in sensibility between my neighbor and myself has been a constant in my mind since the two of us began discussing the current turmoil. I keep comparing her reactions to mine, focusing either on where we agree or where we disagree. Today however, I'm feeling more buoyant. I finally managed to locate her book in a corner of my library. I sat down to read it straightaway and it's shedding light on a lot of things that up until now seemed to me confused and vague.

Tuesday, November 16th

Around ten o'clock this morning I took advantage of a brief sunny spell to go on one of my favorite hikes. It begins just outside my house, winds through the bracken, and ends at a flat rock I like to sit on when the weather is bright and dry. It was all wet today— path, vegetation, rock—but it wasn't raining, the wind had dropped, and a timid sun was trying to break through the clouds. It boded well for a delightful stroll.

Out of nowhere I thought I heard a bicycle bell. A very unusual sound on my island. It's true that here the bicycle is king—I haven't used another means of transport in the twelve years I've lived here. But you never meet either a pedestrian or a motorist, so there's never any need to ring a warning bell.

As I climbed up to the flat rock and turned to look towards the Gouay, I saw in the distance someone in uniform, whom I initially took to be a policeman. It was the countryside warden, who'd been sent by the archipelago's mayor to warn the "population" of Antioch of imminent danger: a radioactive cloud had been detected in the region. The functionary on wheels had no further details for me. He recommended I remain inside, keeping all doors and windows shut, told me not to go out, particularly if it was raining or foggy, and to await further instructions. He handed me a plain envelope containing a handful of iodine tablets and told me to swallow one there and then, followed by one every evening, to prevent lethal radiation sickness.

So it seems the famous beast they've been trying to subdue in order to get it back into its cage is still roaming free. And now it's made it all the way to Antioch.

As the messenger cycled off, I had a strange choking feeling. I was struggling to breathe, as if the air had suddenly filled with deadly particles that I absolutely had to protect myself from—even though just a moment before I had been breathing quite normally. I knew this panic was irrational, but I couldn't stop myself yielding to it. The anodyne, rustic nature of the warden's visit only added to my confusion and anxiety.

I felt like I'd gone back in time eight days, to my initial terror when I thought the world had suffered a nuclear catastrophe. I'd been reassured by what followed, but now the ground was once more giving way beneath my feet. Where had this cloud come from? How had it formed? And what does "radioactive cloud" actually mean? I looked at the sky. It was entirely covered in a bank of cloud. Was there just one suspicious cloud among them? Or was this a figure of speech? Isn't the word *cloud* nowadays merely a handy concept that we use at any opportunity?

As these thoughts were going round and round in my head, it began raining again. And this perfectly banal occurrence was suddenly very alarming, as if it were part of a strategy of encirclement. I rushed home and haven't left the house since.

As I write these lines the rain is still falling, malign and pernicious. The sky isn't spilling water, it's weeping.

*

To ward off my irrational fears, I sat down again with Ève's book.

I'm not reading it the way I might have read it when it first came out, when I didn't know my neighbor, when I didn't have her voice ringing in my ears, and when I knew nothing of her mysterious admirers. I have one nagging question: what is it about this work that swept the friends of Empedocles off their feet?

The theory I put forward a few days ago has gradually transformed into a deep conviction: if Agamemnon has been posted by his colleagues to this out-of-the way corner of the world it can only be because Ève lives here, to keep watch over her and keep her safe during this global turmoil.

As far as the novel itself is concerned, from what I've read so far it seems rather less prophetic than I'd expected. It doesn't predict the arrival of a parallel human race, or indeed any of the things that have taken place over the last week. But it is possible to discern between the lines that the novelist is convinced that humankind has lost its way; that she rejoices in this fact rather than laments it; and that she hopes that "the future"—because it "doesn't live here anymore," as the title makes clear—will one day be controlled by others. What others? Obviously, when she wrote the novel she had no idea. But she repeatedly makes reference to Ancient Greece and even mentions with some affection the figure of Empedocles. A detail that seems remarkable in the light of current events, though I'm sure it went completely unremarked when the book came out. Except, it seems, by the "friends" of the philosopher from Agrigento.

In terms of the inspiration for the novel, it's clearly autobiographical, and Ève makes no attempt to disguise this. Her narrator is called Lilith, the name of the redheaded beauty who according to legend was Adam's first companion, created at the same time as he was and, unlike Eve, not from one of his ribs, which meant she had no obligation to obey him. An exceedingly emblematic, rebellious woman who demands equality in a voice that is calm, commanding, triumphant, and implacable, rather than plaintive, beseeching, or whiny—undoubtedly the way Ève Saint-Gilles sees herself. Which is probably not unconnected to the fact that she had a happy childhood. Her father idolized her, despite his frequent absences, and her mother adored her, even if their roles were sometimes reversed, the disgruntled adult playing the child in the arms of her daughter. From the pedestal upon which her parents placed her, Ève-Lilith watched over them, embraced them, and occasionally admonished them, as if she were the grown woman and they the unruly children, one adulterous, the other adrift.

Her narrator was similarly worshipped by her family, and for a long time believed herself worshipped by her era. Never, since the dawn of time, had women been so little oppressed or submissive; never before had they been invited to free themselves like this from the physical and social corset that had traditionally been imposed on them from birth. Obviously not all women were equally free in every country, and undoubtedly they hadn't completely gained equal rights everywhere, but Ève-Lilith at least felt able to pursue her ambitions, desires, even indulgences, as she saw fit. In her youth, living between Paris, Dublin, Kingston, and San Francisco, she denied herself no pleasure, be it lawful or illicit, benign or risky. She gave her heroine all sorts of adventures, no doubt some of them fantasies, but many must have been drawn from experience. All this would indicate she had no reason to loathe or be skeptical of the era in which she lived. The world she grew up in offered countless of her contemporaries, both men and women, sensory and intellectual gratification that earlier generations couldn't have dreamed of. Holidays to the ends of the earth; tools of communication that did away with distance; ingenious devices to simplify daily life; and constant access to all kinds of music, images, artistic and archaeological treasures—to the entire mass of artworks and knowledge accumulated by our species since the beginning of time. Thanks to new technology, the entire world had become one enormous library, which one could enter at any time, without ever needing to leave the house or even get out of one's armchair or pajamas. For the youthful and nonchalant Ève-Lilith, night owl, party animal, and endowed with a huge appetite for knowledge, it was, quite simply, paradise.

So what prompted the young novelist to predict the tragic demise of this civilization? As I write these lines now, there's nothing surprising about her vision. From the perspective of what's been taking place over the last few days, it could almost be said that her prophecy has come true. It does seem, alas, as though our civilization, despite its spectacular advances, is suffering from an insidious sickness that is leading to its imminent collapse. But it couldn't be seen with a naked eye when *The Future Doesn't Live Here Anymore* came out a dozen years ago. That might explain why it caused such a sensation at the time.

What is this sickness? How to explain how such a dynamic, inventive civilization could end up without a future, and about to be snuffed out? Ève doesn't say explicitly. At least not in the two hundred and fifty pages—roughly two thirds of the book—I've read so far. She probably didn't know against which reef of history men would run aground. But she foresaw the catastrophe, and wasn't fooled by the ambient prosperity.

Around midnight I reached this sentence, *While I was blossoming, humanity was withering,* and stopped reading.

I'll read the rest tomorrow.

Wednesday, November 17ᵗʰ

I was woken at dawn by a call from Moro, who sounded uncharacteristically perplexed, even disconcerted. It was six thirty for me, half past midnight for him. He'd just gotten home from a long evening meeting at the White House.

"The president called us all in to ask the same predictable question: 'Where do you think these people have come from?' I settled for recounting the story I'd heard from you, which is obviously the official version that this so-called intervening power wants us to believe, to lull our suspicions. I was one of the last to speak. I didn't want the discussion to focus on Ancient Greece. I was curious to hear alternative ideas.

"I listened to fifteen people, all meant to have developed reasonable, plausible, intelligent hypotheses, not one of which seemed to me really convincing— not even the one I championed."

Present at the meeting were the heads of the intelligence services, some generals, several members of Congress, and two or three "free agents," as Moro liked to call himself.

"Everyone came into the Oval Office with their own obsessions and their own blinkers. Most seem to believe that Demosthenes is being controlled by one or more countries from 'our' side: China, Russia, India, Iran, maybe somewhere in South America or Europe. I know the person you met on your island swore that's not the case, but that kind of denial only reinforces suspicion."

"I don't want to defend Agamemnon," I felt obliged to say, sounding somewhat sleepy still, to my friend.

"And I can't rule out that he's trying to manipulate me. But if a country on 'our' side, as you put it, has developed the advanced technologies these people appear to have at their disposal, why would they need to resort to such a setup? It makes no sense."

"Don't be so sure. It could make sense. Imagine if the Chinese or the Russians wanted access to US military installations. They'd have the door slammed in their face. Whereas this way a player pretending to be neutral, not involved in any conflict between global superpowers, has managed to obtain the president's assent to intervene on American soil exactly as he wishes. Though having said that, I don't believe in the Trojan-horse theory any more than you do. How could a rival superpower have acquired the superior knowledge necessary to develop a sophisticated arsenal and train a whole group of agents without our intelligence services having any knowledge of it? It's highly improbable. The problem is the other theories are even less likely. A group of people from outer space, say. A theory which four people seriously proposed this evening, including Howard. But that doesn't hold water either.

"You know me, I'm not a man to dismiss a hypothesis before I've thought it through. I do believe that in the future we will encounter other intelligent creatures; it's absurd to imagine we're the only ones in the whole vast universe. But the day this encounter takes place the shock will be instantaneous and extremely violent. Whichever being shows up on the territory of the other will begin with its total annihilation, in order to remove all its capacity to resist; only after it's been conquered will he delve into its art, history, beliefs, and civilization. The notion of people arriving here from another planet, moving into our houses before we even know of their existence, becoming captivated by our history, the Athenian miracle, Empedocles of Agrigento, that seems completely fanciful to me. A charming fantasy born of a philosopher's imagination."

"So you prefer the 'local' explanation?"

"Most of the people who spoke this evening thought it the most credible hypothesis. With one of the usual suspects, the Chinese or the Russians, in the role of 'perverse puppeteer' ... But other possibilities were also put forward. A secret society, a cult, a minority group living on the margins of History, of whom ordinary mortals are totally ignorant."

"Which would fit with Agamemnon's Greek legend."

"Yes, in a way. It remains to be seen where and how such a branch of humanity could have managed to survive for centuries without revealing itself or being ferreted out. Do you really think these people would have been able to develop sophisticated technology and weapons if they'd been living in caves or underground?"

"It's hard to believe, it's true. But in that case who are they? And where do they come from?"

"I don't know any more than you do, Alec. In my view, none of the explanations I've heard so far are convincing. But we must be wrong in some way, because here they are! We still don't know who they are, or how they remained together through the centuries, or why they've suddenly decided to reveal themselves on the global stage. But they're here, they appear to be all-powerful, and it's imperative that we find out very quickly what their plans are for us."

*

At this point in our conversation I told Moro what was being said on the Chiron Islands about the radioactive cloud. Judging by his reaction, he wasn't very concerned about it.

"The same alarmist rumors are going around here as well, but everything suggests they're unfounded. We've investigated a number of incidents over the last few days that seem more serious than others. Not even one revealed levels of radioactivity higher than normal.

"It's not dangerous substances that are proliferating, my dear Alec, it's a state of mind. When Howard announced that our so-called guardians were going to inspect our installations, a lot of military honchos flew into an impotent rage. They couldn't disobey the Commander in Chief, but they had no desire to obey him either. So how did they express their frustration? By telling anyone who wanted to hear it that the 'cleanup' of radioactive substances would be a disaster, and that instead of avoiding another Chernobyl, it would trigger something even worse. Lots of people thought the same, and rumors began to spread and intensify. Here in the US, and in a lot of other places too, I imagine."

"So has anything gone wrong with this clean-up operation?"

"In all honesty, nobody actually knows," was Moro's sheepish reply. "We've no idea what they've done. From what I've heard not all the inspections that took place were at nuclear installations. In fact, that might be just a smokescreen. The claim that a devastating nuclear conflict was imminent and that only the providential intervention of 'our guardians' had prevented a catastrophe was likely fake news."

"To what end?"

"My best guess at this point is they did intervene to carry out a cleanup, but in some other area that's nothing to do with nuclear. Every time Demosthenes spoke to us about the danger, he kept heavy-handedly going on about nuclear weapons falling into the wrong hands, or waste no one knows how to treat. But probably the main concern for him and the others lies elsewhere.

"He kept alluding to research which, if it were to bear fruit, would lead to complete annihilation. That was the word he kept using: the annihilation of the species, the risk of annihilation, instruments of annihilation. And because ever since the Cold War we've gotten into the habit of associating the threat of annihilation with the atom bomb, we fell into the trap. So much so that in his address the president spoke only of the 'nuclear beast.'"

"So do you know what it is that's worrying these people?"

"Not really. I can guess, but I can't be sure. Over the last few days, as far as I know they've gone into almost two hundred sites all over the world, half of them in the States. Mostly laboratories doing research into bacteriology, organic chemistry, artificial intelligence, physics, ballistics. But on the list I saw—which wasn't exhaustive—there were less obvious places, like institutes of agronomy, observatories, several university libraries, a production company that makes underwater documentaries, even—go figure—an old monastery in Kentucky."

"What did they do in these places?"

"I only know the details of one case, a research institute on the outskirts of Baltimore where the son of a friend works. Two women turned up at Reception on Monday morning. In all likelihood they too are friends of Empedocles. The precise moment they arrived, every person in the building fell into a paralysis. As if they'd been gassed. But it seems there was no gas. Maybe some kind of electron beam that produces the same effect. The inspectors worked slowly and carefully. They disconnected the observation and measuring instruments by injecting grains of sand or something similar. They destroyed a lot of files and took others away. And they completely erased all the institute's digital data. There's not the slightest trace of forty years' worth of work, either on site or online."

"What were they working on there?"

"It's a big company with over a thousand employees. They did all kinds of research, had dozens of projects going on at any one time. There was probably only one that interested the inspectors, but they erased the lot, I guess so that no one can figure out what it is they were after."

"Were there any casualties?"

"No deaths, no injuries. There was no altercation. The women did their job undisturbed for several hours and then they left. All while the employees slept. Now they've woken up, but most of them can't move, because their limbs have gone completely numb. They're awake, conscious, not in pain, but unable to move their arms and legs. Doctors have already named this strange paralysis Baltimore Syndrome."

"So the whole operation was carried out by just two people?"

"Yes, unarmed, or kind of. With no weapons, anyway. That seems to be their modus operandi. They're not seeking to impress, either by number or by the materials they're using. Quite the opposite, it's their surprising economy of means that's so stunned their interlocutors. Don't forget, they sent just one man to negotiate with the US government! And they still got everything they wanted.

"You should have seen him, their Demosthenes! When we got back from Chile, after the negotiations had begun in the Oval Office, he compliantly sat where Howard told him to and didn't move. He was always alone, while there were seven or eight of us. From time to time one of us would go out to stretch our legs or eat a sandwich or use the bathroom; sometimes we'd leave in a group of two or three to compare our impressions. He just watched, impassive. He seemed to have no needs, no wants, and nothing to say."

"Did you manage to have another conversation just with him, after the one on the airplane?"

"No. I had to make do with observing him from

afar. It was rather edifying, mind you, and occasionally amusing. There were some memorable moments. For example, Friday night. Demosthenes had just explained that the 'instruments of annihilation' had to be disposed of once and for all, and that the 'friends' were ready to do it. To this end, he asked the president to authorize his people to enter the sites to be decontaminated. 'Which sites?' Howard asked him, quite candidly.

"'That, Mister President, I am unfortunately unable to tell you.'

"'You want us to authorize you to inspect sensitive sites on American soil without telling us which ones?'

"Demosthenes was unmoved. 'If the slightest detail were to be leaked the operation would fail. I'm fully aware that what I'm asking of you is not easy to accept. But if we want to put an end to the risk of total annihilation, that is how we must proceed, there is no other way.'

"Howard looked around at all of us. One after another we all shook our heads. No hesitation. It was out of the question to give these people carte blanche to root around our installations as the fancy took them. 'I must, I'm afraid, respond to your request in the negative,' the president concluded, politely but firmly. 'I'm sure that you would do the same if you were in my position.'

"Ten seconds later there was a knock on the door. A member of the security services had come to inform us that all communications had once again been cut off. Howard stiffly pushed himself up using the arms of his chair and got to his feet. 'I refuse to be blackmailed into continuing these negotiations.' The man replied, 'I understand, Mr. President. Let us adjourn our discussion and give ourselves time to reflect with clear heads.' 'You're trying to humiliate us,' said Howard, and his sadness was not faked. 'You're increasing your threats, your displays of force, you seem to be all-powerful. So why do you need to make a deal with us? Whatever you want to do, do it, and let's not discuss it any longer!'

"The envoy paused for a few seconds before answering. 'It is possible that we will have to act without your consent. I would sincerely regret that. I had hoped that we would be able to establish a relationship of mutual trust. Most of my friends do not agree with me. They have longstanding prejudices against you and all the nations on earth. When they think of your society they see only rapaciousness, greed, a death drive; they believe you to be incapable of using your power for anything other than domination and subjugation; they give you no credit for the principles you proclaim or the commitments you make. They think I am naive, open to be abused. If you tell me there is no possibility of coming to an arrangement, I will leave right away, and you will never have to deal with such an inexperienced and incompetent interlocutor again.'

"He spoke politely, without raising his voice, but it was both a full-scale indictment and an ultimatum. He stood up and began walking towards the door. Howard gestured to him to stay, saying in a voice that was both weary and calm, 'Sit down, my friend; we are doomed to get along.'

"Demosthenes walked up to the president and

placed his hand on his shoulder. 'I am happy to hear this. And I want to continue to believe that we can come to an understanding. But right now, we are all exhausted and on edge. Let us retire and meet again in the morning.' Though he must have been seething inside, Howard managed to keep his cool. He even had the idea of offering the negotiator a room in the White House. We all thought he was going to decline the invitation. But he accepted, saying he was flattered and honored. He was, after all, being treated like a head of state. He was given the Lincoln bedroom, with three members of staff at his disposal. The man spent the night in the White House. You'll notice I didn't say 'slept,' since I have no idea if these people need sleep like we do."

Moro related another memorable scene that took place on Saturday afternoon.

"Howard took a bad turn during the night. His physician, Dr. Abel, stayed by his bedside. Politically, things weren't exactly going well either. We had managed to stand tall, but we had no fallback strategy. They were not going to give up on their 'total clean-up operation,' which was obviously the primary reason the man had come. There seemed to be nothing we could do to dissuade him. Howard joked bitterly, 'I'm no longer Commander in Chief except on paper. I can't order a single bomber to take off, or designate a target to attack. So we may as well believe the declaration of friendship. And since they prefer to act with our assent, we should try and obtain some concessions from them. They have to agree, for example, not to inspect certain symbolic sites, like the White House, the Capitol, the

Pentagon, the State Department, the headquarters of the CIA and the FBI ...'

"We made a long list, which Demosthenes conceded to without argument. With a dramatic gesture, he signed it, stood up to hand it solemnly to the president, and shook his hand. 'We need you, Mr. President, a great deal more than you can imagine. If everything is to proceed seamlessly, with no suspicion or resentment between your people and ours, you must tell your military, your civil servants, your scientists, your fellow citizens, the rest of the world, that this clean-up operation will safeguard not only their future but that of their children too. Have faith and give them faith! We are counting on you, Mr. President, we need your unambiguous and unconditional support.'

"Howard was relatively reassured by this declaration. Given the circumstances, it was the best we could hope for. He nodded his head at each sentence to signal his assent. And so he was furious when the vice president, Gary Boulder, who hadn't uttered a word the last three days, saw fit to ask the envoy, 'And what will you give us in exchange?'

"'In exchange for what?' retorted Demosthenes in a blistering tone. 'We are cleansing the body of poison, and you want us to give you something in exchange?' Then he turned to Howard and said calmly, but with a touch of drama, 'That being said, when the time comes to say farewell, Mr. President, I would like to offer you a symbolic gift in gratitude for your hospitality: I am going to cure you.'

"It was silent as a grave in the Oval Office. Yes, as a grave, though all the talk was of extending life.

Howard grew even more pale, if such a thing were possible. In a barely audible voice he stammered, 'I want nothing for myself.' The envoy replied, 'I am not speaking in the context of our negotiations. It is a gesture of friendship, Howard. May I call you Howard? I have invited myself here, and I hope your memories of me will not be too negative. Like everyone else, I am aware that you are terminally sick, and there is nothing your doctors can do for you now. Our doctors will cure you in one morning.'

"Far from appearing comforted by this claim, Howard looked devastated. 'Be aware that what you have just said will have no bearing on any decision I take as president of the United States.' We were all horribly embarrassed, but the emissary pressed on. 'You are the leader of a great nation, and it is in that capacity that I have spoken to you thus far. But yesterday you had the generosity to call me your friend, and it is as your friend that I am offering to cure you, Howard. Whatever the decision you take about the inspections we'd like to carry out.'

"Demosthenes nodded his head at each of us. 'I think we've said all there is to be said. I'd like to go to my room now, if you'll allow me, and leave you to deliberate. I am sure you would like to address your compatriots, Mr. President, to inform them of your decision. Once you have prepared your speech, my comrades will restore the airwaves so the world can listen.' Then he added, 'One final thing. Would you be kind enough to let me pay my respects to the first lady? She must think I am an absolute boor to have spent all this time in her house without thanking her.'

"After the emissary had quit the Oval Office, the president said in a shaky voice, 'If that man is trying to influence me with the promise of a cure, I wish you to know that it will carry no weight when it comes to making any decisions.' We all nodded politely, respectfully. And obviously, with the utmost insincerity. We glanced at each other out of the corners of our eyes, trying not to smile. We'd all suddenly realized why the man was so keen to see the president's wife."

Moro wasn't sure I'd understood, so he explained with an exclamation, "Just try to imagine Cynthia Milton's emotion when the envoy tells her he can cure Howard's cancer!"

"Do you really think these people can?"

"Demosthenes seemed quite sure of it, and I'm inclined to believe him. His associates have already shown what they're capable of, and I don't think he'd lie or brag about it if they couldn't."

I paused, then said with awe, "If we put aside the political element, for your friend, as a person, this is something he could never have dreamed of, isn't it?"

"Of course, he could never have dreamed of such a thing. But it's terrifying too. The implications are huge. Utterly devastating. You can't imagine!"

Early this morning there was a knock at my door. I had visitors from Port-Atlantique. As I was neither dressed nor shaved, I ushered them in wearing my bathrobe. The three of them couldn't have been less alike, but together they formed a little delegation.

There was old Antonin, whom I often see at La Cap-Hornière and have already mentioned briefly. I've never had a long conversation with him—he tends to converse in monosyllables—but every time I'm at La Cap-Hornière I try to find a seat near him, and it would never occur to me to do otherwise. A long time ago he was the first person to buy a drink for the stranger I then was.

He was accompanied by his granddaughter Gabrielle. She's just nineteen and seemingly unaware of how beautiful she is, a bit shy but with air of determination. It was clearly her idea to bring her grandfather to see me.

And the scruffy young sailor who accosted me last Saturday in Port-Atlantique to talk about Agamemnon had come along for the ride. He was no better shaven this morning, but then nor was I. I learned in the course of our conversation that he's Antonin's great-nephew and that his nickname is *Bouc*, the local pronunciation of *buckle*—maybe it's got something to the with earring in the shape of an anchor he wears in his left ear. He owns the van that brought them over to Antioch. Quite the escapade— it's been years since a vehicle that size has crossed the Gouay.

The elderly man invited his granddaughter to

explain the reason for their visit, which she did with such emotion in her voice that it was difficult to make out what she was saying. I managed to fathom that her fiancé, a sub-lieutenant called Erwan posted to the military base on Fort-Chiron, called her yesterday to tell her he couldn't meet her at the end of the week as planned: all the soldiers had been confined to their barracks because a suspicious boat had been intercepted near the installations, and the man on board arrested. And who might that be? The ferryman! Bouc announced this almost triumphantly, watching me intently to gauge my reaction. I forced myself not to have one.

That evening Gabrielle learned from the fisherman that there had been a brawl on the base and several soldiers had been injured. She tried to call her fiancé several times but got no reply.

"You have to do something," Bouc said to me. "The ferryman's your friend, isn't he?"

"I know him, sure, like everyone does."

"It's never been more than hi or goodbye with me," the young man went on. "But you, he tells things to."

His tone was accusatory. Antonin didn't like it. He took my hand in his in a staunchly protective gesture. His gap-toothed mouth grew suddenly eloquent.

"I have known Alexandre twelve years, and I knew his father sixty years ago, is that not true?"

I nodded.

"You came here from Canada, your ancestors were from the islands, is that not true?"

I nodded again.

The old sailor, who up until that moment had kept his eyes fixed on his hot-headed nephew to try and impose some respect, turned to look at me.

"But the other one," he said, "the ferryman, we don't know where he comes from. If you know, tell us."

I had no idea what to say. If Agamemnon had been with us, I don't think he would have kept his identity hidden. He has never asked me to keep it secret. Yet I'd have felt like I was betraying him if I'd confided what I knew.

"Do you think the ferryman is one of *them?*" Antonin asked insistently.

Could I carry on equivocating? My silence and my evident discomfort had already betrayed me. I thought it best to reply. "Nothing would surprise me these days!"

My words, vague as they were, were understood by my three visitors as a cut-and-dried "yes." I saw them exchange somber glances. I was embarrassed and irritated with myself for not having found a more cautious formulation. But I managed to stop myself from saying anything more, for fear of digging myself in even deeper.

After a few moments of heavy silence, Antonin said in a grave tone of voice, "We suspected so, but we were not sure."

Gabrielle's face was ashen. She had both the fright of a child and the dread of a woman in love. "Do you think he'll hurt the soldiers?" she stammered.

What could I say? Wasn't the situation we were in strange? A lone boatman docks on a naval base, he's arrested, quite possibly at gunpoint, handcuffed, locked in a concrete cell for interrogation. And what do we ask ourselves? Not *What are they going to do to him?* But *Is he going to harm them?* Is an unarmed prisoner going to harm the dozens of armed soldiers who surround him? Even more amusing, dare I say it, is that we ask the question without blinking, as if it were self-evident. In just a few days we've grown accustomed to this aberration; it's already part of ordinary reality.

Overcoming my bafflement, I focused on reassuring my pretty visitor. "I don't think your fiancé is in danger. I don't know the ferryman well enough to guess how he might react to the people who've arrested him. But he's not a violent man, quite the opposite. He won't do anything that might harm the islanders. I'm sure Erwan is not in any danger, and he'll call you as soon as he can."

This time I wasn't irked by what I'd said. I'd redeemed my friend a little, I'd reassured Gabrielle, all while saying precisely what I thought.

Having talked things through with Agamemnon quite often, especially over the last few days, I find it hard to imagine that he or his people could be malicious or bloodthirsty; I'm rather inclined to believe them less brutal, more trustworthy, and more respectful of the fate of the weak than we are. The real problem for me is that they are so powerful that I can't help fearing them no matter what their intentions are towards us.

A comparison comes to mind to illustrate this. Sometimes on a night-time stroll along one of Antioch's trails, I hear the crunch of snail shells beneath my shoes. I'm a sensitive soul, I find these creatures endearing, and I'd never crush them deliberately. But good intentions are not enough to save those in my path. For the snails, my innocent wanderings are murderous expeditions, my innocuous shoes instruments of death. This is what happens when a fragile being finds itself on the path of someone mightier than they.

I held back from sharing such cynical reflections with Gabrielle and the two men with her. I contented myself with telling them that to my knowledge the ferryman's associates have thus far committed no crime, perpetrated no massacre. Nonetheless, had they wanted to, we would have been quite unable to prevent them.

My words seemed to pacify the young woman, and earned me a nod of gratitude from Antonin. Good man! There was such tenderness in the way he seemed to be looking out for the slightest trembling of his granddaughter. As I looked from one to the other, I recalled things I'd been told in Port-Atlantique. It might not be the moment to talk about it, but the story moved me, so I'll make a brief digression here.

*

Antonin and his wife didn't get along and decided to separate—this is going back fifty years or more, when they had two young children, two boys. Rather than engage in endless arguments, the man deemed it wiser to leave his wife the house and all his possessions. According to local legend, he took nothing with him but the clothes on his back. He spent his life moving from one fishing boat to another, avoiding as far as possible returning to the islands, and he never again set foot in the house that had once been his. His ex-wife remarried and his children thought of her new husband as their father.

Was Antonin spineless, irresponsible, fickle? Or had he been too generous? Had he sacrificed his wife and children in order to remain free, or had he sacrificed himself in order not to ruin their lives? Whatever it was, he didn't return to live in Port-Atlantique until he was over sixty. He had become a stranger to his own children. Not even a stranger, given that here on the islands, when you meet a stranger, you greet them with a nod; Antonin's children refused to even look in his direction.

With his own hands he built himself a modest little cabin by the sea and divided his time between fishing—no reason to change a habit of a lifetime—and La Cap-Hornière. He had friends at the bar, he drank, played cards with them, he'd always been well-liked. But sometimes he would stare out of the window, and if he saw one of his sons passing by, or one of his six or seven grandchildren, he'd fall silent and there was no point trying to speak to him again until the next day.

Until the famous occasion a couple of years ago when Gabrielle showed up. Antonin was standing on the pavement outside the bar, shooting the breeze with some mates before stationing himself inside in his usual spot, when his granddaughter appeared from God knows where, walked straight up to him, head held high, jaw clenched, looking like she was about to make a scene. Neither Antonin nor any witnesses to the scene understood what was happening. In the street no one moved, people motioned to each other, stopped themselves from calling out.

Gabrielle opened her arms, then closed them around the old man. She leaned against him for a long time, letting her hair stream over his shoulders. The old sailor didn't move, not even to put his own arms around her. It was like his body was paralyzed, his eyes blinded by tears. He couldn't tell if he was on dry land, or a boat listing off the coast of the Azores.

His son, Gabrielle's father, who happened to be walking by, went right over to his daughter, intent on separating the entwined bodies—a strange scene of love, rebellion, betrayal, and devotion. Once he'd gotten close to them, and was greeted by the small crowd with rebukes and jeers, the man stopped dead in his tracks. Suddenly finding himself ridiculed, he walked away, muttering. Ten days later, he and his brother, dressed in their Sunday best, visited their father in his cabin. Gabrielle had forced them all to patch things up.

Since then, one can well imagine that she occupies a special place, not only in Antonin's heart—he idolizes her—but in the hearts of all the islanders, who hold her in much greater esteem than other people of her age.

As I said, it was certainly her idea to visit me at my home on Antioch. And it was she who eventually stood up and indicated it was time to go.

I pray to Heaven that she finds her lover safe and sound, and that the ferryman has done nothing to dent the high opinion I still have of him.

When I woke up this morning, to stave off my gnawing anxiety I decided not to turn on the radio or
touch my cellphone or computer, and instead to
settle down straightaway at my worktable to draw,
as if the rest of the world were a remote planet. I
know of no better therapy.

Indeed, as I traced sinuous lines in Indian ink my
peace of mind returned, and I managed to sweep my
fears away to a place where I couldn't see them. I was
in a bubble, if I can put it like that, with no other
companion than my favorite character, Groom, "the
stationary globetrotter." I even thought up three
new installments for him.

I'd been sitting at my drawing table for several
hours when the ferryman came in. Outside, the sky
was a dull grey and it hadn't stopped raining. He
entered noiselessly; I only became aware of his presence when I caught sight of his face reflected in a
pane of glass that the untimely gloom had made a
mirror. He was standing there, silent and still. I
waited several long seconds before turning towards
him. Seconds that expressed my disapproval and
surprise.

Until today I'd always greeted him warmly. He's
engaging. Courteous, thoughtful, discreet, cul-
tured, perceptive, pleasant company—I could list
any number of admirable attributes. My fondness
for him hasn't faded at all since the arrival of his
compatriots in this world we thought was ours. By
the mere fact of his presence on the islands, Agamemnon represented a door to an unknown universe

to which he was my only guide. Even if up till now the door was barely ajar, I thought it full of promise. I liked the fact that other world was so close. But since yesterday I've been unable to hold on to that impression. Now I feel as though I've brought an enemy agent into my home.

I made no effort to hide my discomfort, quite the opposite. I wanted him to see it; honesty is a manifestation of friendship, a vestige of trust. Not that I was aggressive or rude. I've never been able to throw someone out of my house, and I couldn't even stop myself from taking the ferryman's hand when he held it out to me; I merely shook it with less enthusiasm than usual, and my welcoming smile was brief.

"It's a bit late for a visit," he apologized.

I didn't reply.

"I can see you're working. I've interrupted you—"

Instead of replying, I stood up from my swivel chair and went and sat in an armchair in the living room. He sat down opposite me. I still hadn't said a word. I looked up at the ceiling, down at the floor. A few leaden seconds went by. Then Agamemnon drew himself up as if he were about to leave and said, "I don't feel very welcome here anymore."

After a moment I replied with a weary sigh, "I would never turn my back on a friend. But the person whose armed exploits I heard about yesterday doesn't seem like the friend I used to know."

"Are you passing judgement on a friend before hearing what he has to say in his defense?"

"Go on then. Explain yourself. I'm listening."

I sat back and crossed my arms.

Seeking permission with a docile look, he picked up a cigarillo from the coffee table. I promised myself not to weaken, and repeated, "I'm listening."

He exhaled smoke first to the right, then to the left, as if performing some arcane ritual. Then he began telling me his version of what had taken place at Fort-Chiron.

"Wednesday morning, three soldiers showed up at my house. They told me the commanding officer of the base wanted to speak to me and had been unable to reach me by phone. Would I mind accompanying them to go and see him? Of course I said yes. I know Rear Admiral Berthelot well, we've met quite a few times, and I've even been to his house. So, having no reason to suspect anything, I went with them. They were in a motorboat; I followed in mine. One of theirs even came aboard with me. Yet according to the rumors going round I was picked up in my dinghy, lurking in a suspicious manner near the military zone. That's what you've heard, am I right?"

"Yes, that is what I've heard," I conceded, and went on in a neutral tone, "What did the commanding officer want?"

"I didn't see him. We moored the boats and the men told me to follow them. They took me to a room with bare walls, sat me down in a metal chair, and left, bolting the door behind them from the outside. They came back a few minutes later. I demanded to speak to Berthelot; they claimed he'd had to leave and had ordered them to hold me there until he returned. I told them I found that very surprising, given that their superior had always treated me like a friend. I said I'd like to go home and would come back to see him later. One of them was an officer who was older than the others, and appeared to have some authority over them. With exquisite hypocrisy he said to me, 'You have illegally entered the perimeter of a military base. You won't be able to leave until you have told us what you came here to do.' Patiently, I told him I had done nothing illegal, I'd come at the request of his colleagues. Obviously I wasn't telling him anything he didn't know already, but I had to say it. It was clear that these young soldiers wanted to know what was going on out in the world, but instead of asking in a civilized manner, like you did, they decided to go about it the hard way."

He smiled at the parallel, and I smiled back. I had no reason to doubt the truth of what he said and felt slightly better disposed to him. But he hadn't yet gotten to the part that most disturbed me. So I said nothing and let him continue.

"They subjected me to a full-scale interrogation: who was I, where was I from, how had I landed the job of ferryman, who was I working for? If I wanted to walk out of there 'on my own two feet,' I'd be wise to 'tell all.' They were trying to get me to admit that I was in the pay of a rival power. They seemed to believe that everything that's happened since last week is some kind of conspiracy cooked up by the Americans, the Russians, the Chinese, or God knows who. I didn't bother to try to open their eyes—the truth has to be earned, don't you think? I told them I didn't know anything more than they did, that they were wasting their time and making me waste mine, and that they'd be best off letting me go home.

"They were not happy at all. They forced me to

stand up and handcuffed me behind my back. It felt like things might turn violent at any moment, and I had no intention of letting them get the better of me. I said, 'I'm not Jesus of Nazareth.'

"'What does that mean?' their leader asked. I said, 'It means that if you strike my right cheek, don't expect me to turn the other one.'

"They all looked at each other and laughed nervously. The man who'd spoken walked up to me and gave me a resounding slap on the face. And just like that, all the lights on Fort-Chiron went out and the entire communication network was cut. My comrades, who had been following every word of the conversation, were poised to act the moment I gave the signal or at the slightest alert. When they saw me being abused, they intervened to get me out."

"How?"

All Agamemnon said was, "As they know how."

He gave me an enigmatic smile to make it clear he wasn't going to say any more about it. But there was no way I was going to be content with whatever he deigned to tell me. I couldn't stop thinking about the visit yesterday from Gabrielle, her grandfather, and her cousin. I was anxious to know every detail of what had happened on the Fort-Chiron base. Very coldly, I repeated Agamemnon's words.

"As they know how."

That was all I said. But it was enough for my visitor to understand that he was going to have to do a little better in response to my legitimate concerns.

"If you really want to know, I'll tell you."

Perhaps he'd hoped I'd be happy with a symbolic victory. Not today.

"Yes, I would like to know."

It was unambiguous. I lit a cigarillo to indicate that I was happy to listen to him talk as long as he wanted.

"Message received." He cleared his throat. "Let's start with what happened yesterday with the soldiers. I'm sure you're keen to know if my people used any devices or materials which could explain the increased levels of radioactivity that the powers that be around here have been harping on about for the last two days. The answer is no, they absolutely did not."

I knew that already from Moro, but I didn't tell him. I simply nodded to encourage him to go on.

"The technique used by my comrades consists of sending out an electron beam—imagine a powerful long-range searchlight, but which emits invisible light. When it's directed at its target, it instantly paralyzes the nervous system, without triggering any long-term side effects. Does that make sense?"

It did, even if I had no idea what kind of technology would make such a thing possible.

"Do you know why they detained you? And if anyone else apart from you has suffered the same misadventure?"

"It seems to have been an isolated incident, the work of a few hotheads. But rumors are being intentionally propagated all over the world, claiming that massive levels of radioactivity have been detected. It's simply not true, either here or anywhere else. It's categorically false. It seems to be a propaganda campaign to discredit us."

I'd heard the same thing from Moro, but I feigned surprise to encourage him to continue. Like my

Washington buddy, the ferryman told me there had been a convergence, perhaps even a consultation, of all those who hoped the "clean-up operation" would fail.

Could this be true? Was it possible that for once all the nations of the world had put aside their rivalries and longstanding suspicions of each other to come together to try and disarm these overlords who are seeking to subjugate them? If that were indeed so, the drama that is unfolding will have in a sense brought us, along with tragedy, consolation. I said nothing of this, obviously, to Agamemnon, contenting myself with an answer that was, I confess, a touch duplicitous.

"Do you honestly believe that the military and ordinary citizens in every country on earth have all swallowed the same conspiracy theory?"

"I hear what you're saying. My theory must seem most unlikely to you. But think about it for a minute! All these leaders are threatened by our arrival. How they would love to prove that we are less competent and efficient than we appear, that we're making terrible blunders and causing untold damage. They dream of seeing us fail and running off with our tails between our legs."

I withdrew into silence. I even resisted the temptation to remind him that his own people had resorted to a similar deceit when they invoked the spurious risk of nuclear catastrophe to justify their intervention.

The ferryman and I bade each other farewell, shaking hands rather more warmly than we had when he'd arrived. Which I was delighted about. I don't like arguing, even when I'm convinced I'm in the right.

Which I think was the case today. He—and by extension they—are accusing us, and we are accusing them. They are making false claims about us, and we are making false claims about them. But the parallel is disingenuous, for we are suffering, and they are not. One day they'll leave as they came, or so they promise. Perhaps this brief proximity to us will poison their minds, but their bodies at least will remain unscathed.

How little they resemble us, our unexpected brothers! They are as like us as we are like Paleolithic man. What would have become of our ill-starred ancestors had we shown up in the caves of Lascaux with our mechanical diggers, tear gas, and searchlights while they were drawing their blood-red animals on the walls? They'd have flung stones and curses down on us, then died of asphyxiation. And we would have declared that they deserved their fate, because their cave was unsanitary and they were as cruel to their animals as they were to their fellow men. *Mutatis mutandis*: that is exactly what is happening to us today.

Curses on our saviors!

Saturday, November 20th

Yesterday afternoon my mouth was filled with the taste of ashes. By evening it was filled with the taste of marzipan and orange-flower water. Not that my fears—for the islanders, as much as the rest of the world—have been swept away, but I feel a lightness of being. The future, by definition, holds death, and so does the past; only the present holds life, as a grape holds sun and intoxication.

Look at me, starting to write like my neighbor the novelist. I'm forgetting myself. I've got to stick strictly to the facts. They're dramatic enough that I don't need to dramatize them further, spectacular enough for me to dispense with stylistic effects and the flourishes of fruity metaphors.

Towards noon, ignoring warnings from the authorities, I set out for Port-Atlantique to do some grocery shopping. I needed to pick up some fresh produce, as well as some store-cupboard staples in case the situation continues to deteriorate over the days and weeks to come.

I'd reached the middle of the Gouay when I heard shouting. Where I was, suspended between land and sea, where the modest cyclist attains the dignity of the tightrope walker, any noise apart from the cries of gulls and the sound of foghorns seems out of place. As I got closer to the other side I could see raised arms, heads, batons, and banners daubed in red paint. I didn't try to make out what was written for fear of slipping on the cobbled path. I had the feeling that if I slipped and fell into the sea no one would come to my aid.

How many demonstrators were out there? Sixty perhaps, at the very most. But on the archipelago, on a November day, aided by the clamor, they gave the impression of being quite a crowd.

Their target was the ferryman's house. I'd be lying if I said I was surprised. It's been brewing since Agamemnon was arrested by the Fort-Chiron soldiers and freed in the way we now know. Even though I had nothing to do with that odd incident, I can't help feeling a twinge of guilt towards this man who is, despite everything, still my friend. I should never have confirmed his identity to my visitors yesterday, even obliquely.

Without getting too close, I watched as people began breaking down the front door and shattering windowpanes, trashing the kitchen garden, throwing furniture out of the windows to excited applause, smashing lightbulbs, and ripping out electrical wires. To tell the truth, I pitied them more than I disapproved of them. The ordeal we've been living through for the last ten days has been all the more nerve-wracking because it has made no sense. And now all of a sudden they have a guilty party! Not a vague suspect, but a genuine, avowed guilty party, one of "them," the only one we'd seen so far, perhaps the only one we will ever see.

This was where I was in my tolerant reflections, when a doubt flashed through my mind. I went up to one of the women standing there wide-eyed and gawking, like me, one of those real salt of the earth types, to make sure—you never know.

"Is the ferryman home?"

"No! If he was, we'd have sorted him out already!"

That was all I wanted to know. The fact that I was on bad terms with Agamemnon didn't mean I wasn't concerned about what happened to him. Now I knew he was safe I could be on my way. But I didn't feel like going to the market anymore, I wanted to get far away from this and every crowd and hurry back to my tiny isle of serenity on the other side of the Gouay.

I didn't rush off straightaway though. A few people had been eyeing me for a while, and I didn't want to give the impression I was running away. Trying to appear unruffled, I began chatting about anything and everything with the person standing nearest to me, alternating complicit smiles with the wry frown of a wise old man. Meanwhile the tone of the cries had gone up a pitch. A group of the most zealous protestors had set fire to the house. In a few seconds it was completely ablaze, as if it had been drenched in petrol. Black smoke billowed out. I still didn't move. Was it a fascination with fire? Or was I afraid I'd be pursued by a few enraged locals who'd once seen me talking to the "enemy"?

Every gust of ash-laden air filled me with shame. Shame at the degrading spectacle. Shame to be standing there, pathetic and scared, unable to show either good sense or disapproval. Shame, too, of my fellow men. I recognized their fear, understood the need to express their disquiet, but this mean-spirited attack on an empty house filled me with disgust.

Eventually I got back on my bicycle to cross the Gouay. No one was going to bother to follow me.

*

If I am to believe my favorite radio station, Atlantic Wave, the alarmist rumors that have been spreading the last few days have now been confirmed: several serious incidents have taken place in different countries at the various sites being "cleaned up," causing damage and injury to both places and people. Atlantic Wave reckons that the events are the result of deliberate activities by our so-called guardians, seeking a pretext to prolong and extend their "clean-up operation." This seems unlikely; it's almost certainly just someone's opinion. But insofar as the radio station's listeners believe it and have done things in response, it can't simply be shrugged off. The wretched scene I witnessed barely more than a stone's throw from my own home was just one of the innumerable manifestations of rage that have been taking place since yesterday.

As far as the maritime zone that lies off the archipelago is concerned, the news bulletin confirms that levels of radioactivity are "back to normal"—a neat formula for setting the record straight without admitting they'd gotten it wrong in the first place. It also said that a number of cases of "atypical paralysis" have been observed among the soldiers on Fort-Chiron. These two pieces of information accord with what both Moro and Agamemnon have told me, so I assume they are correct.

Still, I remain wary and apprehensive. The ferryman assured me that the electron beams his associates deployed to temporarily incapacitate their adversaries are "entirely reversible." At the time I was reassured by this, but now I'm wondering if this paralysis, however "reversible" it may be, might not nonetheless be long-lasting. The next time I see him I'll ask him to be more specific. He's stuck here for a while, even though his home has been destroyed.

*

These developments are preoccupying, to say the least. So why am I feeling so lighthearted? It must be all the champagne I drank this evening bubbling up into my sentences, and the merriment of the person I was drinking with.

I've never seen Ève so cheerful. Everything about my extraordinary neighbor is topsy-turvy; she's exuberant now as the world is caving in and seems near to complete collapse; but I'm quite sure she'll turn taciturn and sulky again if the good life of before were to resume. She has to be the only person left who isn't cursing our supposed saviors. And the mishaps they're accused of? The unfortunate soldiers they've paralyzed? She shrugs it all off.

She was quite right about the radioactive cloud though. Even I'd had a moment of panic when I shut myself inside my house and conscientiously swallowed my iodine tablets, before Moro and Agamemnon opened my eyes to what was really going on; my neighbor, on the other hand, treated this so-called contamination with the utmost disdain. She can barely recall that a "cyclist dressed up as a policeman" had come by and knocked on her door a few days ago. She didn't even bother to open the door to him. She swore to me, laughing, that she shouted down from an upstairs window, "I can't come down, I'm writing!"

I'm happy to believe her, because as far as she's concerned the fact that she is writing is the only piece of news of any real significance from the last few days.

"Thursday I got up early and sat down to write. Yesterday I carried on, and this morning too. I've written fifty pages already. I haven't written three pages in a row in twelve years. I needed this shock, this confrontation. I've found my way, I've found my bearings, I've found my meaning."

"I suppose you're writing about the friends of Empedocles?"

"It's thanks to them I've begun living again. I was imprisoned, and now I'm free. I feel like jumping up and down. I feel like shouting. I want someone to pour me champagne, for the glass to overflow. I want someone to kiss me."

She kept saying "someone," that notoriously inde-terminate figure. I couldn't ignore the fact that the only someone around was me.

Which of Ève's desires should I satisfy first? The kiss? The champagne? I leapt up to camouflage my five seconds of hesitation. I went to the kitchen and fetched a chilled bottle. The cork flew into the grate and nestled among the embers. I took two carved crystal flutes from the cupboard and carefully filled each one. Ève was sitting in her armchair with her feet tucked under her as usual. I leaned over her shoulder and placed my lips upon hers for the length of a breath, then went and sat back down on the other side of the room.

She waited till I was comfortably ensconced and then said, eyes closed, "Nope, you can do better than that."

I stood up again, put my glass on the table next to hers, perched on the wide corduroy-covered arm of the chair, and murmured, "Neighbor!" as if it were a term of endearment.

There were too many lights on in the house. I went round and turned them all off, so that eventually the only light was that of the fire, whose flames had died down but whose smoldering embers cast a radiant glow on Ève's skin. We were in no hurry to press our bodies against one another, we wanted to start with slow murmuring, intense and soft, our eyes closed, our fingers entwined. I supped her voice, her breath, her stifled giggles, her open arms. I smoothed her clothes with my flattened palm as if they were unruly curls. I felt her heart beating in the hollow of my hand.

Every so often the same doubts and questions passed fleetingly through my head—what was reasonable, unreasonable, ephemeral, lasting, what would happen after. But I was elsewhere, I had no body to hear, my mind was ablaze and I had no desire to trade the present moment for sensible thoughts.

Eventually the armchair stopped being comfortable. I stood up and picked up the bottle and the glasses from the table. Ève followed me, barefoot, her hands hooked into my belt. It looked like I was leading her, but it was she who was directing me. First she guided me up the stairs, and then to her bedroom, where she waited a moment while I set the glassware down on the dresser, then pushed me backwards onto the bed.

There was the impatience of desire in her push, but also the rage of triumph. I'd resisted her the other night, pretended not to pick up her hints; this evening there were no hints, it was an imperious demand and the male yielded, gallantly. I may regret it tomorrow, but I don't regret it today. I stole a few hours from the void, I clung to the naked body of my accomplice as one clings to life, until I valiantly ran out of breath.

Afterwards she fell asleep with her head on my shoulder. I couldn't sleep, I didn't even try. Champagne and sex have always had the same effect on me as caffeine. So, wide awake, my head teeming with thoughts, with a great urge to draw and write, I made every effort not to move. I was desperate not to wake my neighbor—how soft and intimate that word sounds when it's murmured into your ear. It has an evangelical, biblical overtone. *Aime ton prochain*. Love thy neighbor.

As I said, I didn't want to wake her. Especially because she told me she's changed her daily rhythm since she began writing again. Day is daytime once more, and night, night. I didn't want the moment of joy we'd experienced together to compromise her other primordial joy: the rediscovery of writing. Even if it meant I'd have to lie like that till dawn, gnawing on words, dwelling on shards of thought, I wasn't going to move.

It was she who moved first. But only after an hour had gone by. She turned in her sleep to reach for the comfort of her pillow. As she did so, I slipped out of bed, very slowly and without making a sound.

I won't deny I briefly considered pulling on my clothes and going home to sleep in my own bed. But it would have felt like betraying her, like stealing a part of the pleasure I owed her. Whether or not it has a future, a night of love doesn't end the same night, like a common or garden-variety burglary. I didn't get dressed. I'm writing these lines wrapped in one of her bathrobes, which turns out to fit me just fine. I took some blank sheets of paper from a ream I found on the dresser and folded them in four to slip into my notebook later, came downstairs, and sat down by the fireplace.

Having imposed the rule on myself never to leave a diary entry till the next day, for fear that events would overlap and the spirit of my journal would be lost, I spent two hours recording the incidents of this long November Saturday, beginning at the ferryman's house in the middle of a riot, surrounded by screams and smoke, and ending here, in another island house, my mind at rest, my body exhausted, and in my mouth, yes, the taste of marzipan.

I've finished writing it all up now. When I see the first light of day I shall brew some coffee, carry it up the stairs, open the curtains and shutters, and then I shall sit on the side of the bed and wake Ève up with a kiss.

Moorings

"Following me in great crowds, they ask me which
path they should take. Some hope to hear an oracle,
while others, afflicted with various diseases, hope for
a word from my mouth that will heal them."
— Empedocles, *Purifications*

Sunday, November 21ˢᵗ

Having not gone to sleep until seven this morning, I didn't get up until mid-afternoon. Just as my beloved is rediscovering the rhythm of the sun, now it is me who is out of step. It's almost like there always must be one person who's awake on the tiny planet of Antioch.

The trouble with reversing my schedule like this is that when I woke up it was already beginning to get dark. Not being able to plunge body and soul into the bright morning light makes me feel horribly melancholic. Tomorrow I'll have to force myself to find my bearings and my rhythm again.

Is it the darkness pressing on my chest today that's altered my mood so dramatically, when only yesterday I was sailing towards joy? Perhaps. But there's also the fact that the new world order makes it hard to imagine a glorious future. Even as I'm exulting in what I'm being offered in the moment, I can't ignore the paramount fact that all of us, I and all my fellow human beings, have become obsolete, destined for cultural and spiritual extinction, or at the very least drastic marginalization. Maybe we'll get something from our masters in exchange; but good God, what could possibly compensate a man for the loss of his dignity?

It was past two when I came downstairs to find Agamemnon waiting for me in the living room, his feet up on the coffee table, my radio in his lap. When he saw me, he stood, removed his baseball cap with polite alacrity, and bowed his head.

"I've come to seek asylum," he said.

He must have marshalled all his skills as an actor to utter those words. He does seem to have some genuine talent, given how he's spent the last two years playing the role of a modest ferryman, and he might never have been unmasked if the world hadn't been thrown into turmoil. But I can't believe a word he says anymore. Of course, I've seen his house being looted and set on fire, the crowd baying for his blood, which might I suppose make his request for sanctuary credible and justified. Though, at the same time, why on earth would a man who's shown himself more than capable of confronting an entire army platoon, and whose people have mine at their mercy, need my protection? And if an angry crowd is indeed after him, how am I meant to protect him? Wouldn't I be just as likely to be lynched alongside him? I bluntly put all these questions to him.

He didn't try to prevaricate.

"Forgive me, Alec. It was a joke. I just wanted to apologize for coming in without knocking and acting like I'm in my own home. I'm a toxic individual now, apparently, no one can have anything to do with me anymore with impunity. I won't stay long."

"Stay as long as you like, the islanders aren't going to ransack my house just because you came to see me. They're not animals. They're scared. Put yourself in their shoes! How could they not be afraid when they've seen the strange paralysis afflicting the soldiers on Fort-Chiron?"

"I wanted to talk to you about that."

"I remember you telling me the effects of the weapons your people use aren't permanent."

"Yes, I did say that, and I promise you it's true. They disrupt the neural signals that provoke a numbness in the arms and legs, but they don't affect the vital organs, and after a while everything returns to normal."

"How long? Two hours? Two days? Six weeks? Ten years?"

"It depends on the individual and the dosage. In the case of the soldiers on Fort-Chiron, I think it'll be a matter of weeks."

"And is there no way of speeding up their recovery?"

"There is a way, in fact, which is why I came to see you."

He stopped. He seemed hesitant to tell me. I didn't want to make it any easier for him, so I said nothing and waited for him to go on.

"My associates are contemplating making an offer."

"To repair the damage?"

"Yes, in a way."

"By doing what?"

"I'll tell you in twenty-four hours."

"I'm not in the mood for guessing games, Agam! If you can tell me in twenty-four hours, there's nothing to stop you telling me now."

"I said twenty-four hours because a decision is about to be made: either we're leaving, or we're staying for a while."

"What does that depend on?"

"My people are debating what to do as we speak. Some are saying we were right to intervene, but that it's time to go. Some regret our involvement but think it's too late to retreat. And some think that whatever we decide long-term, we have an obligation to set right any damage our current incursion has caused."

"And what do you think?"

"I'm one of those who never wanted to get involved. If my point of view had prevailed, I'd still be at my post, an inconspicuous figure in this peaceful maritime environment. I think we were wrong to meddle in your worldly affairs, and we'd be well advised to withdraw as quickly as possible."

"And would you leave too?"

I had to ask, even if I already knew the answer.

"After all that's happened, I have no choice but to leave the archipelago, I'm afraid. I regret it already, bitterly. But it's unavoidable."

I accorded him a moment of compassionate silence before I began questioning him again.

"So, what are your people going to do to 'repair the damage,' as you put it?"

"I don't know yet, I'm expecting a message today. I wanted to let you know that something could happen, soon, and you and Ève need to remain on high alert."

On high alert? What on earth does that even mean? I have no goddamn idea.

He was almost out the door when, trying not to appear overly concerned, I asked, "Are you trying to tell me that Ève and I are in danger?"

"Possibly. But don't worry too much. Both of you will be protected."

*

Two hours later he knocked at the door again and apologized for bothering me.

"I've just been at Ève's place. As we were talking I realized I was worrying you both, even though the whole point of my coming was to reassure you."

I smiled and crossed my arms. "Perfect. Reassure me then. I'm listening."

"I think she has feelings for you."

That wasn't the subject I was looking to be reassured about, though I didn't mind hearing him saying it.

"I like her a lot too."

What made me say that? I had no reason to confide in the ferryman. But the words just popped out of my mouth and I'm not sorry to have uttered them.

Agamemnon grew serious. He seemed moved.

"Ève matters a lot to us, as you know. She has done for years."

I nearly said that she'd only begun to matter to me in the last few days. But this time I managed to keep it to myself, and simply said, "Yes, I'm aware of that. And I get the impression your high opinion has transformed her."

He nodded several times to indicate his agreement and gratification, then added, "And you will have guessed, I imagine, that she is the reason I took the job of ferryman, so I could be close at hand and keep a discreet eye on her."

"Yes. And now you're wondering what's going to happen when you're no longer here."

"I'm not overly concerned," he said. But the way he said it suggested the exact opposite.

Was he going to task me with taking care of her, now I was going to be her only neighbor? But he merely repeated, "She is important to us." Before adding, with a grave expression, "She's alone, fragile, and vulnerable."

Our conversation risked taking a lachrymose turn. I hurriedly changed the subject.

"Since my neighbor matters so much to you, I assume you've told her things I'm not allowed to know."

I was fully expecting denial, or at most a veiled admission accompanied by a warning.

"I answered her just as I answered you. But you asked different questions."

"What should I have asked?"

He smiled politely at my obvious attempt to outsmart him, then stood up, walked over to the glass door, and gazed out at the horizon and the sea. After a few seconds he turned towards me, crossed his arms, and leaned against the wall. He looked like he'd finally decided to speak. I thought I could see the words pressing against his closed lips, making them tremble. But he said nothing. I'd sworn to myself that I'd make him formulate both questions and answers, but it seemed like we were both going to stay silent indefinitely. It was I who gave in eventually.

"How is it," I asked him, "that for so many years, centuries even, we never so much as suspected your presence among us?"

He looked as if he were thinking this through deeply, but I can't imagine my question surprised him in the least, and I'm sure his answer had been prepared long in advance. Eventually he replied, by way of preamble, "We always underestimated the human desire to remain oblivious. If people don't want to know you exist, they'll spend their whole life among you without seeing you. Your neighbor and I," he went on, seamlessly changing the subject, "talked mostly about old Empedocles. She's been interested in him for ages, she even knows some of his writings by heart."

As much to illustrate this as to answer the question I'd just put to him, he began solemnly to recite. *"Like a man preparing to go out on a stormy night who lights his candle away from the wind, so must the fires of antiquity have sheltered in caves."*

He paused, then continued with what seemed like a mixture of suffering and pride, *"And yet, the beneficent flame was cast on but an infinitesimal segment of the earth."*

"Is he talking about your people?"

My visitor shook his head. "Empedocles of Agrigento never knew the men who claimed him as theirs. His fate prefigured ours. He wanted to withdraw from the world, so he threw himself into the inferno. Like us."

The ferryman stopped talking, lost in thought. I had many more questions, but this time I waited for him to emerge from his silence. He spoke slowly, carefully choosing his words.

"Empedocles is one of those rare characters in whom the real and the mythical worlds meet. His name is held by us in the highest esteem, and his sacrifice spoken of constantly. But don't think we take his writings for revealed truth! We quote them often, but in the same way you might quote some lines from Shakespeare or a sentence from Nietzsche, or one of Einstein's witticisms. Having said that, it's true that some of the things he said seem to herald and even encourage our latest venture." And he began to recite again, not without emotion:

> "You will stop the indefatigable winds that rage against the earth and destroy the crops with their breath. Then if you wish it, you will bring forth productive breezes; and after the black rain you will bring forth a drought that benefits men; and after the sweltering drought you will bring forth tree-nurturing streams that live in the ether ..."

Then abruptly he fell silent. His eyes were still gleaming. It was as if he were continuing to recite in his head. Occupied as I was with committing these ancient words to memory, I didn't break his train of thought to ask him to explain them, which allowed him to come back down to earth gradually. Which he did after several moments, with a long, anxious sigh.

"This encounter between your people and mine is not a reunion so much as a collision. No one is going to emerge from this unscathed. There was good reason for our intervention. But in light of the incidents that have already taken place and will no doubt continue to over the next few days and weeks, it would be judicious to bring it to an end as quickly as possible. All we can do now is withdraw in the least painful way. Speaking for myself, I don't want it to drag on. Every new thing we do is going to entrench us more deeply. Every new commitment will incur new resentments. It's a downward spiral."

"I don't understand, Agam. First you tell me that your associates are planning to stay on and repair the damage they've done. And now you're talking about an imminent departure."

"I said I would have liked to leave immediately. But almost all of the rest of us disagree. They have various plans up their sleeve so they will leave you with good memories of our time here."

"Which reminds me, my friend in Washington told me that Demosthenes has promised to cure the president."

"I heard. That's exactly the kind of initiative I meant, and what an abomination it would be!"

"An abomination? To cure a man of cancer, an abomination?"

"Much more than you can imagine. Just look at the uproar we caused when we tried to rid the planet of weapons of mass destruction!"

"That's not the same thing. No nation wants the things that make them powerful taken away. But curing a man of cancer is a different thing entirely. No one would hold that against you."

"Don't be so sure. They certainly will hold it against us. First, we'll be criticized for healing one man and letting others die. Millions of people all over the world are sick with the same disease. Why heal the president and no one else?"

"Good point. Why indeed?"

Before he could reply, his cellphone rang. He held it to his ear and gestured to me that he was going to take the call outside. I motioned to him to sit down and that I would leave the house instead. I wanted to stroll along the island's footpaths while it was still light.

As I made my way towards the nearest beach I went over our conversation in my head. At one point

I sat on a rock to note down the ferryman's words before I forgot them, starting with the quotations from Empedocles.

I should read up on the ancient philosopher, try to find whatever of his writings haven't been lost. Ève will be able to point me in the right direction. Perhaps that way I'd be able to understand a little better the mentality of those who are now governing—or at least supervising—us. Who, if I'm to believe Agamemnon, and despite his own opinions on the subject, don't appear to be ready to leave just yet.

*

I walked back to the house. According to my watch it was five to six. Quietly, I entered my bedroom through the French windows and turned on the radio by the bed to listen, as is my wont, to the main news bulletin on Atlantic Wave.

Have I mentioned that all the events which used to make the front pages have disappeared? Regional conflicts, local news, the economy, sport, even the weather, all are barely mentioned anymore, everything's been suspended. During the entire half-hour news bulletin, the only item that didn't mention Agamemnon's compatriots was a story about a British member of parliament who had suffered a fatal heart attack. For the rest, it was a world tour of the problems at all the sites that have been inspected by the ferryman's friends—a chaplet of strange occurrences, rumors, and confusing predictions.

At one point during the bulletin, I popped my head round the door of the living room. My visitor was still talking on the phone. I shut the door as quietly as I could, lay down on the bed, and lowered the volume a notch on the radio. While I listened to the newsreader, I couldn't stop the myriad questions going round my head. Who was Agamemnon speaking to? Where is this country of Empedocles? Hidden in the heart of our world, or somewhere else entirely? Was he on a local call, or long distance, as we used to say? What language were they speaking in? So many unanswered questions. I'm not going to go through them again, the list is truly endless.

If the strange ferryman with a Greek name and Native American features is indeed about to leave for good, perhaps I ought to get him to reveal a few more secrets before he goes. For, to tell the truth, he hasn't given me more than a few tidbits today. Yes, I have been able to rouse him from his silence, but all he offered me was some riddles and a few sibylline quotations. I—or rather we—have a whole world to discover, a world related to ours, though bearing little resemblance. It's not a few sparse pages of my diary that should be devoted to "those people," but a whole book, an encyclopedia even. But, as the saying goes, the perfect is the enemy of the good, and probably all that's needed for my name to live on is for me to have committed to paper during my short life just a few basic details: *The most substantial information we have about the friends of Empedocles, we owe to Alec Zander, a Canadian-born cartoonist, who ...*

A few minutes later I tiptoed back into the living room. Agamemnon wasn't there, though I hadn't heard him leave. He'd left a sheet of yellow paper on

the coffee table with the terse message: *I'll be back*.
Suddenly ravenous, I headed for the kitchen and
devoured whatever I could lay my hands on.

As I stood at the counter stuffing my face, I felt a
sudden sense of vacuousness and unreality. As if I
hadn't understood a thing about what's been going
on for the last week. Or, worse, as if nothing's been
going on at all. As if it's all been a dream peopled by
ghosts, spawned by my extreme solitude and my
alarm at the ghastly state of the world.

I lay down on my bed and, almost out of spite,
drifted off to sleep, fully dressed. I woke up around
midnight. No sounds around me, no presence, just
my head churning with venomous thoughts.

Monday, November 22nd

I came to terms a few days ago with the fact that from now on our future will be inextricably linked with that of Empedocles. The word *moored* flashed through my mind, but I wasn't sure about using it. There are words like that, that come to my mind, but not my pen. I couldn't conjure up an image. I think in images, drawings, sketches. I've tended to imagine our supervisors up in the air, above the clouds, manipulating from afar the mechanisms of our various technological failures.

I was right not to overuse the word. But today the facts make it necessary. Because now an actual mooring has taken place, albeit discreetly: a floating hospital that, from a distance, might easily be mistaken for a mundane tuna boat. But a symbolic threshold has been crossed. It remains to be seen whether it's one of Empedocles's vessels that is now moored on Antioch, or Antioch that is moored on Empedocles.

I say Antioch, but make no mistake, what I really mean is the whole world. Everything that's happened—all the errors, rumors, accusations, unexplained paralysis, and the rest—hasn't it all simply been a lengthy, underhand process of laying the groundwork to prepare everyone mentally for what's about to happen? A protracted accumulation of pretexts? Agamemnon would deny it, of course. He keeps telling me that his people found themselves caught up in a spiral they never planned and which they soon came to regret.

Spiral? What spiral? It's us, it seems to me, who are in this up to our eyeballs.

It's years since there have been any hikers other than myself and my neighbor on the island's beaches, any piercing sounds other than our raised voices or the shrieking of the gulls, any small boats other than the occasional fishing trawler. There is something incongruous about the presence of the hospital ship, with its crew, equipment, naked mast, chimney, footbridge, lights, and clamor.

Its mission, according to the ferryman, was to get all those—civilians as well as soldiers—who had been "temporarily paralyzed" back on their feet and, if necessary, to treat anyone who'd been contaminated with radiation. An anonymous communiqué, slipped at dawn under the main door of the town hall, was broadcast at noon on Archipel FM, our local radio station. It invited local residents with worrying symptoms, as well as anyone who simply needed reassurance, to come for treatment to La Roche-aux-Fras, on the island of Antioch, on Monday afternoon or Tuesday at any time.

Would the islanders turn up in droves? Would they overcome their distrust and fear and put themselves in the hands of "those people"? At 2 p.m. Agamemnon, at a loose end and somewhat puzzled, came over and asked me if I'd like to try it out, in the absence of any other volunteers. I didn't hesitate. I was motivated less by concern about my health than by curiosity, and also—why deny it—by narcissism. Wouldn't it be gratifying to be the first person to be treated by one of Empedocles's doctors?

The ferryman took me to the hospital ship and deposited me in the hands of a tall, gangly young man with a cheerful expression who answered to the name of Pausanias. No surprise there—another name inspired by Ancient Greece. But this man didn't have Native American coloring. With his height, his thatch of blond hair, and the expression of a child prodigy, he wouldn't have looked out of place on the campus of a Nordic or Canadian university.

He handed me a clear, sweetish liquid to drink, then led me towards a cubicle and told me to get undressed. This evening I'm going to make a sketch of the place, but maybe I should try and describe it here in words: a room shaped like a stretched-out trapezium, walls covered in cork or something similar, furnished with a narrow cot, a cupboard, a chair, a small box for metal objects, and with a rail running right across. On which there was a transparent sarcophagus. The term is hardly appropriate, I know, but it came spontaneously to mind. I'd have called it an incubator if it had been for a newborn. Anyway, clearly I was meant to lie down inside it. As the lid closed the sarcophagus grew opaque and began to slide along the rail and out of the room through a semi-circular opening, into what I imagine was a dark tunnel. I couldn't see or hear a thing. Absolutely nothing. Not a glimmer of light or the faintest sound. I felt a sensation of warmth in my body that at some point began to intensify while still remaining pleasant. The whole thing lasted no longer than two or three minutes, and then I found myself back in the cubicle. I dressed slowly, almost disappointed my adventure was over so soon.

Pausanias helped me out of the sarcophagus. He must have guessed at my disappointment, because he enthusiastically shook my hand and congratulated me on what I'd just done.

"One day you'll realize that you have just experienced the most extraordinary day of your entire life."

I'd like to think so. Logically, today ought to feel momentous. Nothing I underwent could be called banal, neither the experience nor the circumstances. And yet I was no more moved than if I'd had a routine X-ray in a suburban health center. Agamemnon, waiting for me at the end of the gangway, didn't display any of Pausanias's wonderment; he simply asked me if it had all gone well, without resorting to superlatives or hyperbole.

There was still no sign of any other volunteers on the beach. The ferryman duly accompanied me back to my house, then said he was going over to Ève's to invite her to take her turn. I am sure she'll say no. She doesn't like to be interrupted when she's writing; but then again, what wouldn't she do for these "friends" of Empedocles?

I lay down for a few minutes, then called my goddaughter Adrienne and her boyfriend Charles to tell them about my little adventure. Their first reaction was to chastise me for my recklessness. Consenting to being blasted by mysterious rays? How could I be sure my body would withstand it? What on earth had gotten into me, willingly offering myself up as a guinea pig? But after we'd talked for a few minutes, either because they were a little bit ashamed to be scolding a man my age, or because they were intrigued by my description of the hospital ship and the way it was run, they announced they were going to come and see me on Antioch as soon as they could get away. The thing that most intrigued them was the fact that the doctor didn't ask me any questions or try to find out what I might be suffering from. He had zero interest in the specificity of my case.

Two or three years ago Adrienne sent me an article describing how the ultimate aim of modern medicine is an end to examination and diagnosis, and even to medicines and cures; the body would simply go through a "universal treatment apparatus" and anything that was wrong would be healed. I think I even recall that the author of the article called this life-saving machine the "healing tunnel." I realized that was exactly what I'd just travelled through.

What diseases have I been cured of? I've no idea. It's not as if I was ill, as far as I know. Maybe I had some underlying illness, the beginnings of a tumor, or some infection, an ulcer. Does this mean I may have acquired some temporary guarantee against falling sick? I rather hope so. But even if I have, I could still break my neck falling from a cliff or be knocked about by the islanders for consorting with the enemy. And on top of that, if I am to believe Charles, it's entirely possible that my passage through the tunnel hasn't only cured me of an unknown disease, but has also given me a different, more devastating disorder that no one will be able to detect or cure.

What I didn't dare admit to Adrienne and Charles is that since early this afternoon I've had a strange queasy sensation—only intermittently, and for very brief moments—like being slightly drunk, or in the early throes of seasickness.

Anyway, around four o'clock, three cars drew up to my front door and eleven people got out. Old Antonin was there as a guide, and he'd come with a nurse called Benoît and nine other islanders whom I know vaguely, six women and three men, all with symptoms that could in theory be the result of radiation sickness. The expedition had come about in the wake of a fierce but inconclusive debate that was about to continue at my house. Before putting themselves in the hands of these foreign doctors, the islanders wanted to know what I thought. What were the advantages and the risks? I told them what had happened to me and shared not only my own thoughts but also those of Charles and Adrienne.

Agamemnon arrived as the discussion was in mid flow. He was accompanied by Pausanias, which was lucky, I think, for although the ferryman has established polite relationships over the last few years with the islanders, their suspicion of the stranger he's never quite managed to stop being to them has over the last few days turned to downright hostility. Pausanias is no less of a stranger, of course. But there's something about him, something in his smile and his bearing—a hint of naivety, vulnerability, and candor—which makes him seem more approachable.

As soon as he walked in, he turned to each of the women present and embraced them warmly, two kisses on each cheek. He's probably been told this is the local way. He's not wrong, except that the custom here is—apart from young people—we only embrace like that if we already know each other, almost never on a first meeting.

Nonetheless, all these hugs and kisses had a magical effect. The women's nervous tension shattered like an overheated glass lamp. And when one of them, Ernestine, a big-boned, no-nonsense woman who owns the hardware store in town, gave Pausanias's elbow a maternal pat, he blushed crimson like an overgrown child and a battle was won by our so-called protectors that no show of force could have pulled off.

Off we went single file to the beach. And all my visitors, even the ones who'd have sworn that they had only come to support the others, ended up putting themselves through the ordeal of the "healing tunnel."

One after the other, escorted by Pausanias, they boarded the hospital ship. I waited for them on the beach with the ferryman. As they disappeared, a couple of them glanced back at me with a last apprehensive look. Less than an hour later they emerged, slightly disheveled, a bit dazed, crooked smiles lighting up their faces. Some were still combing their hair or doing up their buttons. Suddenly there was a cry. It was Antonin. He stopped at the end of the gangway and waved his hands over his head like a drowning man. I rushed towards him. The others were already standing round him, peering at his hands. He was wiggling his fingers in every direction, bending and unbending them. A miracle!

I should point out here that as long as I've known him the index finger of Antonin's right hand has been crooked and stiff. This minor infirmity is quite common among the islands' sailors; mostly they adapt to it and even pretend to find it amusing, though they know that the loss of flexibility is irreversible and only gets worse with age.

But as he was walking off the hospital ship, Antonin suddenly realized that his index finger had, by some miracle, recovered its former flexibility. He could bend it, unbend it, wave it around, rub his eye.

Was this event trivial, minor, banal, insignificant? Not under the circumstances. Of course, Antonin getting his finger fixed was not like someone being healed in the early stages of cirrhosis of the liver. Except that this hypothetical cirrhosis is invisible to the naked eye, while a finger is visible and tangible. Whatever the healing tunnel might have cured in me and the others, we'll probably never know. Only Antonin's finger bears physical witness.

It didn't take long for the news to travel round the islands, massively increasing the prestige of the doctors of Empedocles. I couldn't understand Agamemnon's odd reaction. When I expressed my admiration for what he and his associates had done, he responded in an exasperated tone that we had to stop going on about this index-finger business.

"If Antonin had gone to see a decent doctor, it'd have had the same result."

This is completely untrue. The finger was arthritic, and no treatment would have restored its flexibility. But I didn't see the point in arguing with the ferryman, who was fretful, angry, and worried.

*

Perhaps the explanation for his reaction is to be found in something he said later that evening: "It's important that these people don't expect anything from us that we can't give them. The worst crises are born of disappointed expectations." To which Ève's poetic reply was that dissatisfaction is the "picture frame of history," and without it history wouldn't be able to proceed in any direction at all.

We were eating dinner around my neighbor's table—Agamemnon, Pausanias, Ève, and myself. Ève told me she had invited the other members of the crew, but they had all declined, some because they had to keep guard day and night, the others presumably either out of fear or shyness.

During the evening I realized from a few dropped hints that the ferryman and my neighbor must have gotten together without me in recent days and talked at length, because every so often I'd pick up an unfamiliar allusion, things they had clearly discussed but not with me. I won't deny this triggered a mild jealousy in me.

No, that's not the right word. I should put it in inverted commas. I have no time for jealousy, which popular wisdom too often dresses in noble clothes. I'm not jealous, just a little irritated at the idea that Ève and Agamemnon have had conversations and are keeping secrets they don't think I'm worthy of.

Maybe they're right. Maybe I am no match for all that's going on around me and my aspiration to chronicle it all. Maybe my vision of things is too lazy and superficial. I'm not saying that as a form of self-flagellation, but I have this feeling there are truths all around me that would be visible if only I had the capacity to see them.

I'm on the edge of an unexplored universe, in the

front row, a privileged witness to an event with no precedent in history, in direct contact with the principal actors, and all I am capable of is being a bystander. The tree is within reach, and I'm just nonchalantly picking windfalls up off the ground.

Rereading the last couple of paragraphs, I realized suddenly what made me write them. Every so often during dinner this evening I felt that slight dizziness, that sensation of seasickness I mentioned earlier. It's definitely either the result of having gone through the tunnel or because of the liquid I drank before the treatment. I didn't mention it to Ève, Pausanias, or Agamemnon, and it's possible they didn't notice anything amiss. I didn't show any sign I wasn't feeling well, I just sat there quietly, forcing myself to focus on their conversation. I hope to God it's just a passing wobble. It would be quite normal for a treatment as new and unusual as this to unsettle me for a day or two. Tomorrow, when I wake up, I'll know if my head and stomach have calmed down. I can sort of smile about it now, but if this queasiness turns out to be lasting, I won't be smiling anymore.

Charles and Adrienne are right to think me reckless. I'm pleased they're on their way here. I need their youth, their keen eyes, and their sound instincts.

Tuesday, November 23rd

Antonin's index finger isn't Cleopatra's nose, but he'll have his fifteen minutes of fame nonetheless. I foresaw it in what I wrote yesterday, though I hadn't yet gauged the scale of the phenomenon. There's been a surge of arrivals since dawn, anyone with any kind of condition, visible or not; everyone with something to be treated.

Not that the Antioch beach has been transformed into a freak show. There aren't any lepers or strikingly maimed people, no Elephant Man–style protuberances. A crowd of sick people, yes, but people who are sick like you and me, suffering pain, discomfort, a dose of hypochondria, or simply the effects of aging. Everyone seems to have a rendezvous with hope on this grey autumn morning in the tiny hamlet known as La Roche-aux-Fras—the *fras* or *fradets* being, in the local argot, creatures of legend known elsewhere as *fadets*, *fadettes* or *farfadets*, with a proclivity for miracles and tricks of perception.

Never have so many of the inhabitants of Port-Atlantique made their way over the Gouay. As soon as it opened, they crossed in a long cortège, knowing they would only be able to return at 4.15 p.m., at the next low tide. There must have been at least thirty cars on Antioch today, dozens of mopeds, and a forest of bicycles. In total around a hundred and fifty patients went through the now famous "healing tunnel." The rest waited their turn in vain; they shall have to come back tomorrow.

The local radio station covered the event live, and a television crew came over from the mainland. I was interviewed as a resident, and I complained, politely of course, about the crowd disturbing the tranquility of my island.

To be honest though, none of this really affects me. Of course, I couldn't bear it if my haven were to become a permanent fairground. But once in a blue moon I can cope with being caught up for a few days in a bit of a hullabaloo.

I was amused, proud almost, when Moro called me from Washington to tell me that he'd just heard Antioch mentioned on the TV, and they'd even broadcast images of the island. *Ventre-de-thon!* as the old salts say round here—*Goddamn tunny tummy!* It's become my favorite profanity.

The main reason for this burst of interest is obviously the arrival of Empedocles's doctors. "My" beach is one of twenty-seven places around the world where their floating hospitals have anchored. This number of simultaneous moorings is not insignificant; but at the same time, twenty-seven coves scattered over the entire surface of the planet isn't very many, and it's extraordinary that my piddling little island should be one of the very first destinations.

The other reason for Antioch's sudden fame is the rumors of miraculous recoveries that have been spreading like wildfire. To a rational mind there's nothing palpable apart from Antonin's finger; but there are people now who swear, without waiting for more evidence, that the tunnel has cured them of gout, cirrhosis, kidney failure, tumors, and many other unpleasant ailments.

And if the skeptical still needed a public demonstration, they got it this morning on the beach in front of the gathered crowd.

Some wheelchair-bound soldiers from the Fort-Chiron base turned up, pushed by able-bodied friends, relatives, and colleagues. The incident took place at around ten o'clock; one of the young soldiers who had been exposed to the paralyzing rays also had a broken leg, and Agamemnon tried to prevent him from going through the tunnel, under the pretext, I was told, that the plaster would damage the instruments. At which point Pausanias turned on his compatriot, caustically lecturing him in their language. No one around them said a word, but it was clear that the ferryman was no hero for trying to stop the soldier from getting treatment.

It was Pausanias who eventually prevailed. He cut off the plaster with a portable electric saw, then escorted the patient into the cubicle. When the young man emerged a few minutes later he was walking normally. His fracture had gone. There was scattered applause. There was something evangelical about the scene, the way all those who witnessed it were filled with wonder. Apart from Agamemnon, I suppose.

I wasn't there when the incident took place. I heard about it from Gabrielle, Antonin's granddaughter, who came to see me with her fiancé Erwan, who was back on his feet after his own trip to the hospital ship. The two young people thanked me for supporting them during their ordeal. To be honest, I hadn't done much and they owed me nothing. But I could tell they didn't want to hear me say that. What had just happened was to them a marvelous event, and it would have been odd for me to deny all responsibility as if I wanted to wash my hands of the whole thing. I told them I was happy that everything had turned out well and I'd be delighted to see them again one day.

Gabrielle and her soldier beau weren't my only visitors today. From morning till night, my house served as the hospital ship's waiting room. All day long I handed out coffee, cider, and wine, gave reassuring opinions, and listened to anecdotes, secrets, concerns, and the overused maxims that people round here have such a fondness for.

After twelve years living on the archipelago, I know them all. None surprise me anymore. When an old sailor is about to undergo open-heart surgery, there's a good chance he'll declare, "I'll be good as new!" I must have heard this expression a dozen times today, spoken in the usual tone, but it doesn't sound the same now. It's not a cliché anymore. Everything indicates that our new guardians' medicine does indeed make everything "good as new" rather than being merely a treatment. Hasn't this been the dream of mortals since time immemorial?

*

Moro called me again today and we had a long conversation about this very topic. I say "this very topic" because our conversation focused specifically on the contemporary desire to prolong life at any cost, to remain eternally young; an aspiration that was presumably less talked about in the old days when medicine promised so much less, but which today, as he said, threatens to become all-encompassing and even, paradoxically, destructive.

It was nearly 2 a.m. in Washington, but my friend was still up. He wanted to know if excitement was mounting on the islands because of the "miraculous" cures taking place on Antioch. I told him that while there was some excitement, there hadn't really been any miracles; not much had happened other than old Antonin's finger and the soldier's leg being fixed. My inclination to minimize the significance of these cures pleased him but didn't quiet his unease. He seemed to me to be exaggeratedly worried, and a little obsessed. Perhaps it was his insomnia, but also perhaps because he has an eagle's eye for things both past and future which I've never had. I only have one skill, that of being able to seize the moment and capture it, preferably in Indian ink. Things that have yet to take place are opaque to me; at most they trigger some confused foreboding. Moro, on the other hand, can predict, anticipate, extrapolate. He can project himself intellectually weeks, months, even years ahead, and thus assess the likely stances of different protagonists.

During our lengthy telephone call today, he kept going back to the question of these cures. He kept getting me to repeat that the whole thing was much ado about nothing, and then he'd tell me that on the contrary the fate of the entire world depended on it.

But the contradiction was only apparent; the way my friend flushed out the hidden import of a subject was by reasoning through a series of paradoxes. Rather than contradicting him I usually follow him down these meandering paths, harnessed to his reflections. I might prompt him occasionally, but without hindering his thought processes or distracting him. That's why, I think, we remain close, despite our geographical distance.

During our conversation, he told me that President Milton had decided to forbid the floating hospitals from operating in the United States or on their territorial waters. Moro approved. "There's no doubt that with their help we'd have been able to accelerate the recovery of the people afflicted with this strange paralysis. But they're improving anyway. It'll take a bit longer if we treat them ourselves. It's a minor irritant, largely insignificant when compared with the major irritation of yet another intervention by our so-called guardians. Howard's been under a great deal of pressure, but he's holding strong, and he's been proven right. The public is behind him. Americans like to depend on their own strengths, and they love being asked to make sacrifices. There's a big humanitarian and patriotic movement to aid the victims."

"It's all for the best then," I said sarcastically, for I detected in his voice an anxiety that seemed to contradict his reassuring assessment. But if his response confirmed my suspicions, the way he put it nonetheless took me by surprise:

"It certainly would be all for the best if it wasn't for all these 'miracle cures' taking place all over the world, including on your island. The media interest is intensifying, and I can't help but fear the worst. At the beginning they talked about it like those so-called miracles in Sardinian and Cretan villages, all church candles and women swathed in black. People are used to tales like that, they know which corner of the brain to store them in so they don't think about them except in moments of personal distress. But in the current circumstances, I'm very worried about all this chatter. If my fellow Americans are willing to be convinced that all they need to do is to climb into a machine and they'll come out the other side three minutes later, cured of all their ills, God alone knows what might happen. It could be the end of the world—and I'm weighing my words carefully."

"Wait, Moro, I'm not following you. You said 'if,' but the machine really exists. I've seen it. I've been inside it!"

But he was undeterred.

"You told me that you'd been through what you called a 'healing tunnel.' But you still haven't told me what you've been cured of."

"I don't know."

"Exactly. Maybe you've been cured of something. Maybe nothing at all. Am I right?"

"In my case, that's true, as there wasn't anything obviously wrong with me, yes."

"You see, there is a doubt. That doubt could be our last chance. We have to maintain it as long as we can. Otherwise all will be lost."

Why is this healing business bothering him so much? He didn't explain right away. But a little later in our conversation—which lasted a good thirty minutes, I'm just reporting snippets here—he spelled it out.

"Howard is not well and he's getting worse. He's been utterly depleted by what's been going on. Last September his doctors gave him another couple of years to live, now they're talking about a few months at most, maybe even weeks. In light of what's been going on since yesterday on your island and in various other places around the world, how can I not think of the banana skin that Demosthenes dropped behind him when he left the White House?"

"You're talking about his promise to heal the president?"

"He first mentioned it to Howard, in my presence, and later on to Cynthia, who was hardly going to be unmoved by the idea, and she's now putting increasing pressure on her husband to accept the offer. With every day that passes the question will only become more persistent: will the president of the United States of America agree to be treated by 'them'? Howard is fully aware of the symbolic significance of such a decision and is standing firm. It's only because he's refusing to be treated by them that he's able to ban the floating hospitals from berthing anywhere along the US coastline. But how much longer can he face them down?"

*

Towards four in the afternoon, after my house was finally emptied of visitors, everyone in a hurry to cross the Gouay before the tide came in, I was seized by the desire to see Ève. I was dying to know what she made of all the hubbub on our island, the two concurrent "invasions," that of the hospital vessel, and that of the crowd waiting to be treated.

My charming neighbor was sitting in an armchair in the living room, whisky in hand—a familiar image. But she was not alone. Agamemnon sat facing her in the chair it has become my habit to sit in. If I can talk about habit. He looked concerned, serious; I might even say grief-stricken. She, on the other hand, looked utterly unfazed. She was glowing, if not actually ecstatic. She wore an impish expression that made her look very young. Is it because she's writing again that she seems so invigorated? Or is it because she's sleeping normally now? Could it be the effect of her journey through the healing tunnel yesterday? Only the way she was sitting, with her legs folded beneath her, holding her glass up to her temple, reminded me of the person she was ten days ago.

What had they been talking about, my uncommon friends, that had made Ève so cheerful and Agamemnon so glum? I was sure it was something to do with the incident that had taken place alongside the hospital ship.

"I heard there was a scuffle this morning?" I said to the ferryman. "Apparently a young soldier in a plaster cast turned up and you tried to stop him being treated."

"Yes, that is sort of what happened. You've been correctly informed." I waited for him to go on, but he said nothing more. I persevered: "I'm bemused by your attitude, Agam. Just yesterday, your people were considered enemies here, which seemed to upset you. All the world's ills were being blamed on you, you were nearly lynched, your house was set on fire. Today the islanders are starting to see you all as heroes, saints, saviors. You should be feeling pretty good, optimistic, proud even. But no—you seem more put out than ever. What's bothering you so much?"

My tone was perfectly friendly, but Agamemnon was reluctant to tell me. I think he was trying to catch my neighbor's eye. When he failed to do so, he sat forward in his chair with a look of resignation.

"Don't you see what's happening? Hundreds of people are thronging to the ship. Another couple of miraculous recoveries like yesterday and today, and the entire population will be queuing up at our door. I'm not too worried about it here, we're on an island, we're linked to the rest of the archipelago by the Gouay, and without regular traffic from the mainland we can still control the flow; even if all the islanders demanded to be treated we could complete our mission in three or four weeks and leave. But what about elsewhere? A number of floating hospitals have been dispatched to various places around the world to cure the people who've been afflicted with paralysis or who think they've been exposed to radioactivity. If there are cranks everywhere like Pausanias offering willy-nilly to heal people and spreading rumors of 'miracles'—"

So that was it. Like Moro, the ferryman was worried about rumors. I was about to mention their shared fear, but I caught myself just in time, and let him spell out his position.

"Do you know how many sick people there are on earth? Billions! Everyone falls ill at some point, grows old, dies; we can't mend the whole world."

"But if you could, why not?"

"Alright. Supposing we have the knowledge to cure every disease, how long would it take us to treat every sick person, one after the other? If we mobilized all our hospitals, all our teams of doctors, we could treat ten, maybe twenty thousand a day, at the very most. We never planned to deal with such numbers. It would take us centuries! Is that really what you're suggesting? That we stay here till the end of time?"

"You could at least train our physicians so they could carry out the task themselves."

"You mean furnish them with equipment? Show them how to make it? Or set up new medical schools for you on every continent, take over the training— is that what you want? Don't you see where we'd be heading if we did that? First our medicine would supplant yours; then you'd discover that your science and technology are out of date, and we'd have to send you all our scientists and teachers. Your schools and universities would gradually become satellites of ours. A downward spiral, and this time it would be permanent. Our people would mix, our two worlds would become entangled for good. Your civilization would melt away and ours would become unrecognizable."

Ève looked rapt, as if this possibility, presented by the ferryman as apocalyptic, filled her with immense joy.

"I'd like to live for a long time, just to see it," she

said. "The definitive dissolution of our civilization!"

The way she said these words, they had a dulcet, seductive timbre. I didn't think it worth responding. I looked at her for a few seconds with a discreet shrug of bewilderment before turning back to Agamemnon.

"All this chaos because you fixed a sailor's arthritic finger and a soldier's broken leg?"

"All this chaos because of charitable types like Pausanias, who can't say no!"

"How could he say no? If a physician sees a sick person and knows what to do to heal them, isn't he obliged to? It's a question of ethics. They can't say, 'There are too many of them, I'm only going to take the oldest, or the youngest, or the sickest.' And they certainly can't say, 'I'm only going to cure my own people.'"

"We came here with the express purpose of treating those suffering from paralysis and radiation sickness, and we should have stuck to that."

"Well, it's too late now, people are beginning to find out what your medicine can do for them. They aren't going to let you go now."

"It's never too late. All we need to do is take the decision to leave. We could be out of here in an hour."

"Let down all the people on the beach and simply disappear without an explanation?"

"Yes, disappear, just like that, using whatever pretext we choose. It would be the lesser evil in the end. To begin with, people would beg us to return. But they'd give up eventually."

"They'd curse you!"

"No matter. Let them curse us if they must, it's of no importance. The only thing that matters is that we get away from here as fast as possible. Regrettably, many of my people are reluctant. There are others like Pausanias. I love that young man like a brother, but he annoys me deeply. He is happy to do good but when it ends badly, as is often the case, he can't conceive of the possibility that it might be his fault. A wise man knows he's responsible for his actions and their consequences; a man devoid of wisdom thinks he's merely responsible for his intentions."

"So if it was up to you you'd leave tomorrow?" Ève interrupted, a glint of feminine reproach in her eyes.

"Not tomorrow, today. Stop looking at me like that, both of you! You'll see soon enough, it'll be you criticizing us for not having left sooner. We came to prevent mass annihilation and nothing else. Every additional thing we do will only poison your lives and ours. Forever. Until the end of time."

*

When I got home I found my goddaughter and her boyfriend waiting at the front door—which I'd locked for the first time in years. They'd had some trouble crossing the Gouay. All the motor vehicles that had driven over to Antioch this morning began leaving in single file all at the same time, afraid of being caught by the high tide. If Adrienne and Charles had tried to come by taxi they'd have found themselves stuck on the other side, the traffic was so dense. They rented bicycles in the port instead, but with so many cars the crossing was tricky and they'd walked some of the way to avoid being knocked off their bikes.

"When there's a traffic jam on the Gouay, the earth really has been knocked off-kilter," said Adrienne, only half-jokingly.

Wednesday, November 24th

I don't know how many times in the last week I've felt as if the world has changed to the point of being almost unrecognizable. And I'm feeling it again this evening, because of something that in the past would have only stirred up the kinds of people who like to stalk grief and show off their sensitivity—a domestic drama entirely driven by the fear of losing a loved one, but which threatens to change the face of the earth.

Moro keeps cursing the "blindness of women." I've certainly known him better disposed to them. Now he genuinely seems to think that because of them our entire civilization is on the verge of collapse.

Ève, of course, is gloating.

Still, today began well, with the assurance that the situation was coming under control. According to repeated rumors broadcast by various media outlets—whose source was quite obviously the White House—Milton was about to launch a global diplomatic offensive targeting international leaders, aiming to encourage them to follow his example and refuse to allow the floating hospitals on their territory. As for those that had already berthed, contact between the Empedocles physicians and the local population was to be as limited as possible.

Within the US administration, and specifically the armed forces and national security agencies, there is hope that the incursion of our so-called guardians will soon be seen as no more than a parenthesis; this strange page will be turned, and we will return to the previous world order in which the United States is still the world's superpower. This desire to turn back the clock might seem fanciful, but it isn't completely inconceivable, considering that the friends of Empedocles keep repeating that their involvement in our affairs is only temporary, and that they never had any intention of allowing it to drag on. As someone fortunate enough to have direct contact with them through the ferryman, I'm pretty sure Milton's initiative wouldn't have displeased them, because it would have given them a chance to extricate themselves without being accused of non-assistance to victims.

I say "would have" because the president's diplomatic offensive came apart at the seams before the end of the day, and in the most unexpected way. To be fair, Moro predicted it days ago, and suspected it would happen. But for the vast majority it came as a huge surprise and shock.

It was the moral equivalent of a thermonuclear bomb—forgive me for the hackneyed comparison, but unfortunately it's the only one that comes to mind at such a late hour.

The "bomb" took the form of an interview with Cynthia Milton, broadcast on one of the main American TV channels.

"Howard is dying," said the first lady. "His physicians say he has no more than a few weeks to live. I don't want to lose him, and I think it is irresponsible of him not to be doing everything he can to defeat this cruel disease. I believe he is sacrificing himself out of a sense of duty and honor. He does not want his personal suffering to lead him to make a decision that might not be in the American people's interest, and would do nothing to further the cause of global peace and understanding. But I refuse to allow him to sacrifice himself. It would be an injustice—to me, to our children and our grandchildren, to all those who love and need him. It would be a form of suicide, and our faith reviles suicide, it is a crime against God. I call on every American wife and mother to support me and help me convince Howard to change his mind."

The call was heard, instantly. In the hour after the interview was broadcast, in cities across America, thousands of people, mostly women, went out into the streets brandishing hastily scrawled placards begging the president to agree to treatment and do all he could to ensure that everyone suffering from an incurable disease would receive similar treatment from the doctors of Empedocles.

The movement grew and grew throughout the day. It was like a kind of civil disobedience sweeping the entire nation. The administration was stunned. By the end of the afternoon the White House was forced to publish a communiqué announcing that President Milton, "sensitive to the opinion expressed by his beloved wife and a large number of her fellow citizens," had agreed to treatment "on condition that every American with a terminal disease like him is treated in the same way," and "having made clear to the emissaries of the intervening nation that in the event of his recovery, it would have no impact on his political decision-making."

I called Moro just before I sat down to write about it. He sounded very depressed.

"Just as the White House spokesperson was finishing up reading the communiqué, Demosthenes told us a floating hospital had already moored southwest of the capital, on the Washington Channel, parallel to the Potomac River. There's some kind of marina there. I have no idea when or how the ship had reached here, nor why our coastguard failed to spot it. I guess for the simple reason that from the outside it looks just like any other cruiser. Anyways, Howard was flown there straightaway in a helicopter, accompanied by Cynthia. Right now, as we speak, the president of the United States of America is in the hands of these people, lying naked inside a glass sarcophagus and no doubt being blasted by strange particles."

I said my friend sounded depressed. Devastated would be a better word. I thought his reaction was somewhat excessive.

"Why would it be the end of the world if the president of the United States allowed himself to be cured of cancer thanks to a more sophisticated medical knowledge than we have? Is it just a question of wounded pride?"

"Believe me, no, it's not. Not that pride shouldn't be taken into account in international relations. But what I'm afraid of goes well beyond that. If people believe that someone or something—an individual, a group of people, a political party, a cult—could cure them of all their sickness and suffering and prolong their lives, they'd worship them, become their willing slaves. The person who controls the length and quality of a person's life is, quite simply, God. Which means that this strange nation, whose existence two weeks ago we had not the slightest idea of, is on the verge of being deified. Not some distant, hypothetical deity who barely lets itself be glimpsed, who encourages doubt to linger, but a deity materially present among us."

"Hold on. I take you to task for one exaggeration, and now you're launching into another one that's even crazier."

"You think I'm exaggerating? Listen to me. Tomorrow virtually every human being on earth will be bowing down to these people, calling them their lords and masters. Our entire civilization has both feet in the grave. You go ahead and write its epitaph."

*

Here on Antioch, today might have seemed much like yesterday, in the sense that the archipelago's inhabitants began to arrive in large numbers as soon as the Gouay was passable, queuing patiently in their vehicles to reach the floating hospital. Whenever a seriously ill person appears, everyone lets them cut in line and then looks out for them to emerge so they can see their transformation. That said, the most miraculous recoveries are not necessarily the most spectacular; everyone cheers the disappearance of a simple fracture, but someone who'd been at death's door might still be brought out on a stretcher, arousing no more than a small gust of whispers, though for all anyone knows they've been granted a second chance at life.

At dawn Adrienne and Charles went to La Roche-aux-Fras to observe the phenomenon. They returned deeply disappointed. The deserted beach was strewn with greasy paper and empty cans, just as at the end of an ordinary summer's day. The floating hospital had cast anchor and sailed away from land for the night and was now waiting for patients to arrive before returning to shore. From a distance, there was nothing remarkable about the vessel at all.

Disappointment turned to cynicism when the ship eventually moored and my young friends approached it to offer their services as physicians, only to be informed curtly that there was no place for them onboard other than as patients.

Adrienne tried to maintain her sense of humor. "We felt like Native American healers offering our services to a great white doctor." But Charles was seething with rage. "They're humiliating us on our own land. They'll regret this."

I tried to console him. "You should know that some of them feel trapped by what's going on and want to leave as soon as they can."

I thought about what Agamemnon had said. I wondered if he was the person the young couple had spoken to.

"What did the man look like who turned you away?"

"What did he look like?" said Charles angrily. "They all look the same to me."

I didn't insist.

Thursday, November 25th

When I began keeping this journal, the incidents I was writing about were on a scale I could deal with. They were happening consecutively, which meant I was able to observe, evaluate, and analyze them while also assiduously exploring my own frame of mind. Now I find myself being assailed every minute by hundreds of pieces of information, all directly related to the events that originally inspired me to write the journal, which I now feel obliged to turn into an exhaustive and comprehensive chronicle of global upheaval. But I'm not up to the task, and I'm quite tempted to throw in the sponge and go quietly back to my paintbrushes and Indian ink.

However, I've made it a rule since I was a child never to abandon either a project or a cat I've begun to feed. It's the only strategy I've found that enables me to conquer my tendency to apathy and indifference.

So as long as I'm at liberty to do so, I shall carry on. I'll listen, take notes, record, verify. The only difference is that from now on I'll have to make a strict selection of what I record. My paragraphs won't always seem to follow on one from the next. But there's always a link, of course. Because everything happening all over the world is part of the same phenomenon.

*

Since early this morning I've been feeling like the entire world will soon resemble my beach here on Antioch. Out of nowhere, hundreds of floating hospitals are now in operation on the shores of all five continents. I don't know how many there are exactly, since no one is bothering to count them anymore, just as no one is drawing up lists of the men and women queuing for treatment at the bottom of the gangways. Most of the time they wait in orderly lines, but there have been periods when it's been chaotic; according to reports there have been several altercations that have periodically obliged the Empedocles physicians to suspend the treatments they're carrying out and move a little way from the shore to wait for things to calm down.

Notwithstanding these confrontations, the queues are growing longer. And, of course, the so-called miracles are multiplying; there's no indication that the appeal of the healing tunnels will fade for a while yet—for a very long while yet, if I'm to believe what Moro told me when I called him this afternoon for news of Howard.

"We don't know. They treated him and then released him. He was taken straight to Bethesda where they're doing all sorts of tests to evaluate the impact of the treatment he received. We're still waiting for the results. I hope for his sake he's in the clear, but even if he is, it won't allay my fears at all. If the White House announces tomorrow that the president has recovered, the whole of humanity is going to race to the floating hospitals. Already now—"

"You're not wrong. It'll be madness for quite a while. But it'll calm down eventually, no?"

"Oh Alec, I wouldn't be so sure. It's not ever going

to calm down. Even if our so-called benefactors were able to treat 600,000 patients a day, those queuing hordes would still be here in forty years. We'll be watching the same spectacle till the day we die."

Again, he was saying the same thing as Agamemnon, almost in the same words. With the same tone of frustration and fear. My response was glib. "Till the day we die, you reckon? In forty years' time? Forget it, young man. With the new medicine these people have brought us, you and I are going to live at the very least another hundred and fifty years."

My quip was uttered in the heat of the moment as a bid to temper the effect of my friend's implacable argument with a smile. But I heard my own words, and they took my breath away, left me speechless. It took me several long moments to compose myself.

"What do you reckon, Moro, how long do you think they'll be able to extend our lives?"

His answer was furious. "What's the point of living for a hundred and fifty years if the world has ceased to belong to us?"

I understood he was on edge, but I didn't know all the reasons why. It turns out there's been one specific thing playing on his mind, which I was completely unaware of. When he eventually decided to confide in me, it was of course primarily because of our friendship, but it was also partly to explain the severity of his earlier words, and the failure of his sense of humor.

It hasn't yet come out, though it won't be a secret for much longer. He sounded distraught. "No one could possibly criticize Howard for agreeing to be treated. But he's made an unforgivable mistake. Stupid and unforgivable. I've tried to dissuade him but he's as stubborn as a mule, he won't listen to anyone, not even Cynthia."

There was a silence. I was careful not to break it. I had to allow my friend the space to change his mind and not let me into his confidence. But, at last, he went on.

"When a president undergoes surgery under a general anesthetic, the convention is that he sends a letter to the speaker of the House of Representatives and the president of the Senate to declare that he will be temporarily incapacitated and is therefore provisionally transferring his powers to the vice president.

"This wasn't required in Howard's case, because at no point was he going to lose consciousness. But he insisted on following protocol, arguing that the treatment he was going to receive involved an element of uncertainty and therefore the Constitution must be followed to the letter.

"In accordance with the same text of the Constitution, the twenty-fifth amendment, when the president comes round, he must send a second letter to the same recipients stating that he is now able to resume his duties. This has happened three times in the last fifty years, and each time the president has returned to his duties the same day. The longest interruption lasted no more than eight hours.

"Howard ought to have sent the second letter yesterday evening. He did not. Nor has he done so today. He has still not signed it. This means that legally, as we speak, Vice President Boulder remains acting president, and Howard is still, strictly speaking, incapacitated. When anyone asks, he responds that there is no hurry, he needs time to think. But I'm beginning to fear the worst."

"You think he's considering resigning?"

"Yes indeed, that's what I'm afraid of."

"But why would he want to?"

"The real reason is he feels guilty. He agreed to be treated because he couldn't resist the pressure from everyone around him, but he feels it is nothing less than a betrayal of his oath of office. He thinks he's been morally blackmailed by Demosthenes, which means he's compromised his capacity to make judgements based solely on the national interest. It's true it was a horrible dilemma for him, and also for his friends, myself included. How could I advise him to let himself die? It was out of the question! But it's also absolutely the case that by accepting medical treatment from a rival power's physicians—I won't go so far as to call them occupiers, but at the very least they're present on our nation's soil without having been invited—he has compromised his legitimacy when it comes to decision-making." Moro sighed deeply. "So here we are. I don't know how we're going to get out of this impasse. For once I wish that Howard was a cynic, with no moral scruples. But he's not."

Moro's dismay was all the greater considering his low opinion of Vice President Boulder. As Milton's health had been deteriorating, Moro had increasingly expressed, beyond his grief at the thought of losing a friend, alarm at the thought of seeing the country fall into the hands of a man he considers a real bad apple.

How ironic that should Boulder become president it won't be because of Milton's death, but because of his likely recovery.

*

Now I've detailed Moro's political concerns, I think it wouldn't be out of place for me to mention that it's not only in Washington where the arrival of the floating hospitals is causing commotion—right here on the island of Antioch their presence is bringing its fair share of drama.

I saw it again this morning in the eyes of my goddaughter and her boyfriend, who appear increasingly upset, humiliated even, by the situation. After they'd been shooed away by the Empedocles physicians, they decided to go and offer their services at the Port-Atlantique health center. They found it completely deserted. No patients or medical personnel. Our own health system, not so long ago our pride and joy, has been utterly forsaken, like a carrack from the Middle Ages in the era of the steamboat.

I suggested the youngsters make the most of their enforced idleness to take a break after an exhausting year and reflect calmly on the current goings-on. But they're already talking about going back to Paris, imagining perhaps that the death throes of civilization will take longer to play out there than elsewhere.

Only Ève is still in good spirits. Everyone else—at least whoever has shared their thoughts and feelings with me: Moro, Agamemnon, Pausanias, Adrienne, Charles, as well as some of the islanders I've talked to over the last few days—is, without exception, unnerved by what is happening. Everyone but Ève. She has retained intact the same aura of beatitude she's had since the ferryman told her of the existence of those strange visitors who like to call themselves the friends of Empedocles. She believed in them straightaway, committed herself to them, and hasn't wavered one iota since. She repeated it this evening when I went to see her.

"Let's face it: it's not like our civilizations have been massacred by cowards, they've simply gone bankrupt. We've shown ourselves to be incapable of guiding the reins of our carriage, because we're heading straight for the wall. Isn't it a godsend that other hands have taken control?"

I don't believe as she does that the people of Empedocles are "heaven-sent," but overall, I don't disagree with her analysis. It's clear that the world has long been adrift, and that we appear to be incapable of avoiding the coming calamity. She may express herself rather brusquely, but she isn't wrong.

What's more, she is completely transformed, physically and mentally, to the point of having become a living image of what she believes. When I first met her, she was lackluster, now she's radiant.

She used to be despairing, and now she could breathe hope into the whole of humanity.

How to resist the urge to believe her? How to resist the urge to love her?

Today, humanity has experienced an escalation of hope. But it's a perverted hope. Putting those two words together perfectly expresses the paradox of the present moment. Our desire for eternity has become our path to servitude.

See, now I've begun talking like Moro, even though yesterday I thought he was being immoderate. It's true that events have swiftly proved him right. Humanity is out of control, and I can't see now what it might cling to in order to break its fall.

The fateful episode that's making me talk like this took place on the island of Grenada in the Caribbean Sea, though it could have taken place in any number of other places. A floating hospital in a marina, a short distance from the other boats. A long line of people waiting on the dock. Women holding babies, sick people needing support, the odd person in a wheelchair, a few groups of boisterous kids treating the occasion like a holiday newly added to the calendar. It was an unruly crowd, and no one apart from those standing right by the gangway leading up to the hospital ship was paying much attention. There was a television crew filming the scene.

Suddenly, around noon, there was uproar. Some local worthy or neighborhood mafioso tried to force his way with his bodyguards past a group of teenagers. There was lots of yelling, shoving, and confusion. Then shots, a burst of machinegun fire. Screams. Another burst of gunfire. People ran for cover behind parked cars. On the deserted quay lay three young men and a slightly older woman. All four with terrible wounds, lifeless, likely dead.

The police arrived and stood in a cordon around the victims. Then a mother came and threw herself onto the body of one of the young men, and other family members did the same. There was the sound of wailing. In three minutes, the mood on the quay had utterly changed.

According to local journalists and eyewitnesses I heard interviewed on Atlantic Wave, at first the Empedocles physicians did nothing to intervene. They retreated inside the vessel and seemed to be preparing to sail away from the coast if they were threatened. But quite quickly they reappeared in their white coats, bearing stretchers. Eight of them walked over to the bodies. The police let them through and the families moved aside. The wailing died away and silence fell.

It didn't take long for pious lips to begin their feverish muttering. People were behaving as if a miracle was already taking place. Calmly, the four bodies were lifted onto stretchers, carried up the gangway, and taken on board the floating hospital. They disappeared from view. An hour went by and then the four Lazaruses reappeared. They stood waving and scanning the crowd on the quay for familiar faces as if they'd just returned from a holiday in Trinidad or Jamaica. They hurried down the gangway and were met by their families on dry land.

Everyone took a few seconds to react. First there was murmuring, muffled and cautious speculation, people huddling, shaky, in the arms of the person next to them. Then there was scattered applause, but mostly from the younger people present. The adults were mesmerized. Many fell to their knees, weeping tears of joy and fear.

Of course, it didn't take long for the news to make its way around the world. Now everyone is eagerly awaiting similar episodes; for days now, people have been talking about nothing else but miraculous recoveries, no one is even surprised anymore, and I don't think I've heard a single commentator express doubt as to the veracity of the story. I rather get the feeling that universal common sense—if there is such a thing—has swapped sides; now not believing in miracles is unreasonable. Which is beginning to get on my nerves, I must say.

I ought to put the word *miracle* in quotation marks, given that there's nothing truly miraculous in what I've just described, no dark forces or anything supernatural, just the results of highly sophisticated scientific knowledge. But it's turned us all into wonderstruck primitives.

I was about to call Moro to tell him about this incident, but I changed my mind. I know only too well what he'll say.

I exchanged a few words with Adrienne, saying that I found the term journalists were using, *resurrection*, excessive to describe a recovery so shortly after death. *Resuscitation* seems more appropriate, I'd argue. She agrees, but only partly, telling me that her colleagues like to talk about a resurrection even after a minor heart attack. That said, and whatever the terminology, there's no doubt that the immediate and complete recovery of four victims of bullet wounds pronounced dead at the scene is evidence of the existence of medical expertise incomparably superior to our own.

I was able to have this conversation with my god-daughter because finally she'd decided to stay with me instead of returning to Paris with Charles, as originally planned. They had a row this morning. It's possible they haven't been getting along for a while. But it's also possible that their quarrel had something to do with what's been going on. Ever since their arrival, I've been aware of their divergent responses to the people of Empedocles. Charles is furious at the very thought of them, while Adrienne shows a lively curiosity. She wants to know more about their enigmatic history and their scientific advances, while he just wanted them to leave as soon as possible; three times I heard him say he "just wants them to get the hell out of here."

In any case, I'm delighted that Adrienne is staying, and that we'll be able to listen to the news together and discuss what's going on calmly over dinner.

*

If there was any doubt in our minds about the overwhelming superiority of the medicine of the "others," it was swept away this evening in the most eloquent and resounding manner, in a communiqué from Dr. Abel, the president's oncologist. After a few paragraphs, peppered with technical terms and statistical comparisons for the benefit of professionals, he concluded with the following lines, which expressed both the noble modesty of the scientist and his overriding dismay:

As far as I can tell, President Howard Milton no longer presents any symptoms of the serious illness he had been previously diagnosed with. His overall health has improved remarkably, and his life appears to be no longer in danger.

The knowledge I acquired during my years of studying and practicing medicine is insufficient to allow me to understand the process by which this full recovery has taken place. For this reason, I have decided to cease all my professional activities in this domain. I have handed in my resignation to the board of the Bethesda Naval Hospital, with immediate effect. I have also requested that the president and Mrs. Milton no longer consider me their personal physician. I will never forget their tremendous courage during these challenging years. But, listening to both my instincts and my intellect, I know that morally I no longer have the right to continue treating patients using knowledge that has become obsolete.

The disillusioned introduction with which I began today's diary entry was inspired by Abel's statement. The observation made by a superstar oncologist that his branch of medicine has become obsolete might well, I fear, be extended to our entire civilization.

Of course, if we take a step back, we could try to put the incident in perspective. Throughout history, people have seen their civilizations become obsolete. Every time a traditional culture has come into contact with a more powerful and sophisticated society, a portion of humanity has experienced a kind of ending of their world. The example that keeps coming to mind is the arrival of Europeans in the Americas in 1492. But there are others. One might argue that over the last few centuries many non-Western societies—India, China, Japan, the Muslim East, sub-Saharan Africa—have seen their medicine, and arguably all their traditional knowledge, fall into disrepute and then gradually be forgotten.

The difference is that up until now, when one of our civilizations lost power, creativity, glory, prestige, and dignity, all that was salvaged by another. Never, until now, has the entirety of our humanity suffered such an all-encompassing loss of prestige. And never, to my knowledge, not even in the case of the Aztecs, has the blow been so sudden.

Having reread the last couple of paragraphs, I've changed my mind. First of all, I wonder if I'm jumping too hastily to conclusions in assuming that the decline of our medicine is synonymous with the rout of our entire civilization. My instinctive sense is that this is indeed the case, but I'm too tired right now to evaluate things calmly and in detail.

These nocturnal misgivings are without a doubt the vestiges of my training as a lawyer; I don't like the idea of drawing half-baked conclusions that a more exacting colleague could easily demolish.

Abel's communiqué made me wonder something else: if a highflying American physician feels humiliated by the crushing superiority of the intervening power's scientific knowledge, how might a proponent of alternative medicine—an acupuncturist, homeopath, witchdoctor, or shaman—react? It's a question that deserves, I think, to be put more broadly: if the fate of the world has been taken out of the hands of the wealthiest and most powerful nations, will this grievance be experienced with the same levels of alarm in Mexico, La Paz, Calcutta, Kuala Lumpur, or Dakar as in Washington?

What I'm wondering, if I'm honest, is whether the vanquished of history, the "left behind," won't be tempted to react ... a bit like Ève, convinced for so long that the table of the world has been badly laid, and now gloating as she watches it being brutally tipped over and the most prosperous guests unseated from the top table.

Some evenings I find myself toasting the collapse of our bloated, arrogant civilization, so obviously messing everything up yet always convinced we're right. But to be honest, mostly I join her out of politeness and because I'm fond of her, not out of conviction. I love the life I've made for myself—my tiny island, my drawing and writing—and all this upheaval is scaring me.

*

I have one final observation to record tonight. I've seen multiple references in the media to the fact that Howard Milton has yet to officially resume his duties, meaning that Gary Boulder remains acting president. Some commentators have expressed surprise and bemusement, but I haven't seen any speculation about the potential resignation of the head of state.

Given the no doubt highly justified fears that Moro has expressed to me, I can only assume that the affair will gain traction in the coming days. On second thoughts, it's very surprising so little has yet been written about it over the last twenty-four hours.

I'm beginning to discover things about Empedocles and those who brag about being his friends. It's not much relative to all the things I don't know, but with patience and tenacity I've gathered every scrap of information I can lay my hands on, so maybe I shall manage eventually to piece together this hidden side of our history.

Am I even right to say "our" history? Are these people part of our world and we theirs? I can't even say yet if our two civilizations really do share a common origin in Ancient Greece, or if that's just a myth. Nor do I know if our so-called guardians ever intervened in centuries past without us knowing. What I can say, without much risk of being mistaken, is that the next episode of our history is not going to come about without them. They are going to be part of it, whether by consequence of their presence or their absence.

Our two rivers, each for so long having followed its own course, have now merged into one. One way or another from now on their waters will always be mingled.

*

I woke up this morning with a single thought going through my head: I had to talk to Pausanias, to get him to tell me everything that Agamemnon has refrained from telling me. Specifically, to ask him about their medical knowledge: what stage it's at in the eternal struggle against disease; what age they can live to; and whether it's true that it can get the better of death.

I went to the beach and somehow, despite the mayhem, I managed to find him and make him promise to come for dinner. He kept his word, and after this evening I feel a little less ignorant than when I woke up this morning.

But before I report what the physician told me I must note down some developments that I've observed during the last two days.

The Empedocles vessel is not the only boat moored at the beach here on Antioch. There are thirty or so other boats of all different sizes. There's even a cruise liner, too huge to berth, that cast anchor a nautical mile from the coast, groups of whose passengers are being ferried over on lifeboats—a word that's now taken on an unusual meaning—to join the lines of waiting patients. The stream of people, along with all those crossing the Gouay, is beginning to cause chaos. It's bearable for the time being, but if the stream becomes a flood, and worse still if it continues like this for years as Moro predicts it will, it means the end of my precious solitude.

Nothing could be more anxiety-inducing for me. Despite all that's been going on, I'm still able to live the way I want and to recount the wrecking of our civilization. It goes without saying that I'd lose my peace of mind if my tiny ark were to sink. Is this selfish? I'm sure it is. But my selfishness is fair enough, given that it's my survival that's at stake.

All over the world, innumerable people hope to be able to enter the healing tunnel. Thanks to the combined effects of President Milton's spectacular recovery and the so-called resurrections on the island of Grenada, the frenzy of my fellow humans has increased by several degrees. Currently, in every country, rich or poor, in every town and village—except perhaps for a few rare communities living completely on the margins of our flagging civilization—there is not a single person of sound mind who hasn't heard about the miracles accomplished by their medicine, and who doesn't dream that they and their loved ones will benefit from it as soon as possible. Every time the presence of a hospital ship is signaled somewhere along the coast, endless columns of vehicles form along the local roads.

As I've already noted—though it bears repeating and highlighting—all over the world, normal life is now on hold. Workers are no longer working, students no longer studying, governments no longer governing, consumers are consuming only what is strictly necessary, and even the crime rate has plummeted.

In the coming days I'm sure I'll have occasion to give some eloquent examples of this worldwide disruption. For now, I simply want to record the inexorable rising of the tide, and register my disquiet. Before returning to Pausanias.

*

He turned up at my house just before eight o'clock this evening. On the advice of Adrienne, I'd prepared a vegetarian meal. She claimed that such an advanced civilization as that of the friends of Empedocles would almost certainly have renounced the practice of killing animals to feed their bodies. When questioned, our visitor confirmed that he didn't eat meat or fish but without saying why. I have the impression he's made it a rule not to criticize the practices and beliefs of the indigenous people that we are.

There were going to be four of us around the table, but this afternoon Ève canceled, explaining that she had some unexpected visitors and would try to join us later in the evening. She didn't come.

It was Adrienne who fired off the first sally once we'd sat down to eat, with the simplest, but in the circumstances the most telling, question of all.

"How old are you?"

Our guest paused before answering. I thought at first it was just because he was working out how to say the numbers correctly in our language. But perhaps he was nervous. Whatever the reason, he stammered slightly as he answered.

"Ninety-two." He seemed embarrassed. I thought for a moment he was going to apologize. For what? His extraordinarily youthful appearance? I'd have put him at forty at most.

"I knew your eyes would widen, because you are not accustomed to associating an appearance like mine with such an advanced age. But this is the result of an evolution that has nothing miraculous about it, your own society is familiar with it. Imagine a painting from the seventeenth century. A man who isn't even fifty years old with a physiognomy that to your eyes is more like that of a man of seventy-five. I'm thinking of some of Rembrandt's self-portraits. The age a person appears to be evolves along with medical progress."

"So what is the life expectancy for someone of your age?" asked Adrienne.

"I cannot tell you precisely. We can now delay aging and extend life expectancy, but we do not know to what extent. We do not yet have the necessary perspective."

"You mean you people no longer die?" I asked.

"Generally speaking, those who agree to regular medical checks cease to age. That does not mean that they will not die one day from something undetectable that we are as yet unable to treat."

"If I've understood you correctly, some of you don't want your lives to be extended?"

"It happened sometimes at the beginning, because there were failures. People whose arteries we managed to keep young but whose brains we were unable to keep from deteriorating. We have improved the process now."

"So no one dies anymore?"

"There's the occasional fatal accident, but it is very rare, and it is considered an absolute tragedy. Much more so than for you, infinitely so. Of course, you mourn when a person dies young, or after a period of terrible suffering. But because you know it is inevitable, you accept it. In time the age of the deceased loses its significance, and their suffering is forgotten. The mourners in turn will die and their grief will be buried with them.

"But when death becomes something that can be

avoided, as it has for us, behavior changes. The idea of risking one's life doesn't have the same meaning; it is no longer simply about knowing if one will die a bit sooner or a bit later. It means something much more significant, and a person would be mad to take that chance.

"Actually, there has been a similar evolution with your people as well. Once advances in medicine meant that it was no longer usual for people to die at forty, for women to die in childbirth, behavior changed; human life became more precious, and now you want to preserve it at any cost. Even in military conflicts you would prefer that no one died."

"It's rather sad people don't want to risk their lives anymore," I observed. A bit cheeky of me really, given that I've always been at pains not to risk my own. I've never gone in for diving, parachuting, or abseiling.

Pausanias nodded his agreement, and then added, "Happily, this evolution among my people, which could have made us cowardly and timid, is compensated for by another consequence of our medical advances: our ability to repair. If a man is so paralyzed by the fear of dying that he dares not so much as lean out of a window, he can force himself to be brave by reflecting that if he falls it is highly likely that his life will be saved and he will come round entirely unscathed.

"That said, I do think our medical advances have made our people awfully cautious, meaning their lives can sometimes be quite boring. Without the dance with death, life loses its tragic dimension, it simply does not have the same appeal. The sense of being mortal is the basis of the desire for liberty, and the raison d'être of philosophy and art. That is why I have such affection for your people, with your fears, fleeting happiness, and short-lived rebellions."

As if to dispel any possible misunderstanding, he added hastily,

"We all share this same affection. Which explains why we judged it vital to intervene now, whatever the consequences."

"Was the risk really that serious?" asked Adrienne.

"It was, yes," Pausanias answered, with a somber expression that he hadn't had up until now, which made his face suddenly look less young, less cheerful—perhaps even less innocent. "Imagine for example a deadly virus spreading with dizzying speed, but those who catch it show no symptoms for several weeks. By the time it's discovered it's too late, no one can stop the spread, neither your physicians nor ours. Entire populations will already have been infected."

"Does such a virus already exist?" I wondered.

"I hope not. But there are people trying to develop one. And if we are not careful—"

He looked like he was about to say more, but abruptly he got to his feet and looked at his watch.

"I have to get back to the boat. We are working all the time now, day and night, to deal with the crowds. I have very much enjoyed having a break, but now it is over."

I stood up in turn and drew out of my pocket a piece of paper on which I had jotted down the words of the philosopher Empedocles of Agrigento. I'd first heard them quoted by the ferryman, and now I had a sudden urge to recite them in the presence of his compatriot. Why? I suppose I wanted to keep him there for a little longer, or to get some kind of reaction from him. It wasn't anything calculated, I was being impulsive. Marking with a pause where I thought the line breaks came, I read out loud:

> *You will stop the indefatigable winds that rage against the earth*
> *And destroy the crops with their breath.*
> *Then if you wish it, you will bring forth productive breezes; and after the black rain you will bring forth*
> *A drought that benefits men; and after the sweltering drought you will bring forth*
> *Tree-nurturing streams that live in the ether.*

Pausanias applauded with an amused look on his face, and said, in a tone that was meant to sound mysterious, "The quote is correct, but incomplete. Is that how Agamemnon taught it to you?"

I was intrigued. "I thought I'd written it down word for word."

Now it was Pausanias's turn to recite:

You will learn what drugs are for what ills, and what to do against old age,

I alone shall teach you this, to you alone will I give this power.

You will stop the indefatigable winds that rage

Against the earth and destroy the crops with their breath.

Then if you want it, you can bring forth productive breezes; and after the black rain you will produce

A drought that benefits men; and after the sweltering drought you will produce

Tree-nurturing streams that live in the ether.

And you will bring back from the Underworld the strength of a dead man.

There were only the most miniscule differences in the lines I had quoted, undoubtedly due to translation, and the line breaks were almost the same too, but the ferryman had clearly cut the lines at the beginning and the end, as if he were censoring Empedocles. Pausanias guessed what was going through my mind.

"You must not hold it against your friend, he is terrified by the turn of events. The idea that billions of people are going to flock to us, gather at our ships begging to be treated and to help them avoid death, it terrifies him because he sees the end of our ordered and peaceable civilization. I am of a different school of thought; I have always regarded your history with more"—he groped for the word—"*enthusiasm* than distrust. But today, with all that is going on, I must admit I am no longer sure about anything."

He did seem rather jumpy. He glanced again automatically at his watch. "I really do have to go."

"I'll walk with you," said Adrienne, grabbing her coat.

The night air was colder and crisper than usual, and I thought of going with them, but then I decided I should leave the youngsters to themselves.

Disappearance

"Let there be always at our door
This immense dawn called the sea."
Saint-John Perse, *Amers*

Sunday, November 28th

I hadn't finished writing my diary last night when the lights went out. I had to complete the entry by candlelight. This morning the power is back, but the radio waves have been blocked again. There's no internet or cellphone coverage, and the monotone whistling on the radio has started up again. The floating hospital that was moored on Antioch appears to have suspended its activities, sailed out to the open sea, and disappeared from sight. However, if the many people who were still lining up last night are to be believed, our noble healers have sworn to return.

Right now, I can't say if they're going to keep their promise, or if they just wanted to calm the crowd for fear that their departure would provoke desperate scenes. Have they sailed away from the coastline to consult? Or have they gone for good, like old Empedocles, leaving as their legacy a lead sandal on the edge of a volcano? Have we witnessed the abrupt separation that Agamemnon has been pinning his hopes on? I don't know. The ferryman has also disappeared without saying goodbye. Nothing remains of him but the charred ruins of his house.

Writing these disillusioned lines, I can't help wondering if I'm penning an epilogue: they came, they triumphed, they blew a wind of fear and hope over the world, and now they've gone.

My goddaughter is much more shocked than I am. Last night, as she walked with Pausanias back to the ship, she diffidently confided her desire to help him in her capacity as a physician; she recognizes that she can't aspire to the status of a colleague, now that her medical knowledge is obsolete, but she hopes she might be useful, and wants to learn whatever she can from them. The old-young man told her he was prepared to allow her to board the hospital ship tomorrow. Firstly, she would go through the healing tunnel, and then she would assist him with patient relations; at some point in the future she would be allowed to get involved in actual medical procedures.

At no point did he indicate that the ship was about to weigh anchor. Adrienne is convinced he knew nothing about it, that he must have received his orders during the night. She's still hanging on to the hope that the hospital ship will return and she'll be able to go on board and gain some knowledge about their medicine.

Ève shares her hope, and even goes further, behaving as though the friends of Empedocles haven't really left. She trusts them implicitly. "If they've once again withdrawn from the eyes of the multitude," she said to me, "it's because they have good reason to; and if they've decided to make us suffer, it's because we deserve it." Didn't Moro say that our "saviors" were going to become our gods? Well, here she is, the new religion's first priestess!

A radiant priestess, I have to admit. When I think back to the jaded, bitter, lackluster woman my neighbor was just a fortnight ago, I can hardly believe she's the same person—this isn't the first time I've noted this, but I'm constantly astonished. They have literally transformed her. The passage through the healing tunnel has given her not only the complexion of a young woman, but the allure, bearing, and voice to go with it. Even more than that, this rebellious woman is positively reveling in the spectacle of our fellow humans' and civilization's humiliation, as if it were a revenge, or a personal triumph.

She wholly identifies with the people of Empedocles and seems proud of them in a way that she never has been of her own. Witness what she said to me this evening, in a rather grandiose tone that I found slightly grating:

"Agamemnon explained to me why it's vital that their path doesn't get mixed up with ours."

"And why is that? Enlighten me."

"Because we have uncontrolled impulses, recurrent fears, age-old hatreds, persistent archaisms, and if we were to gain access to the knowledge they have acquired we'd use it to kill each other and end up destroying every society on earth. That's why they took so long to reveal themselves."

"So how long were we to have remained ignorant of their existence? Till the end of time?"

"Until the day came when the encounter between them and us wouldn't have been dangerous anymore. All through the centuries their dilemma has been the same: if they were to contact us, what kind of relationship should they forge? Ought they to treat us as equals, as brothers? Share their knowledge with us? We'd have abused it, turned every one of their discoveries into an instrument of destruction or enslavement. So what should they do? Treat us as their inferiors? As eternal children? Keep us in a state of subjugation and oppression? That would have been a betrayal of their own ideals."

"Ève, for the love of God, spare me this masochistic nonsense. Do you realize what you're saying? That these people have always held us in contempt, and deservedly so; that they could never have imagined treating us as equals; that they have no choice but to subjugate us or abandon us. You can say it in your sweetest voice; it won't work. You're insulting me, and yourself."

"But it's not about you and me, it's about the multitude."

"Wake up, Ève! We're part of the multitude!"

"Ah no, not me! I've always kept my distance. I've always dreamed of something else. I've constantly been hoping that one day I'd be delivered from this horrible relationship with men. And now the miracle's taken place. My longed-for saviors have finally turned up. I'm not going to deny myself this pleasure. Haven't you noticed how happy I've been since they got here?"

"Yes, I have."

"Thanks to them, I've begun to love life again. You can't hold that against me."

"I don't."

"Good." As she said this, she literally fell into my arms. I was sitting in my usual armchair. She was standing next to me, extolling the wisdom of our guardians, and then without warning she simply dropped down as if the chair were empty. I held her to me and kissed her on the forehead, then her lips, whispering, "Child."

She didn't seem to mind being called that; she cuddled up to me even more, burying her face as she might have hugged her father when she was a little girl. We stayed like that for a moment, a long, delicious moment of my breath against her bosom.

Sitting on me, she weighed nothing. And when I got to my feet she was still in my arms, still weighing nothing. I realized then, like an epiphany, that my passage through the healing tunnel has had a restorative effect on me. Not that I've acquired Herculean strength, but I seem to have recovered both my muscle strength and my lung capacity from thirty years ago, which is miracle enough for me.

How strange that it's taken me a week to become aware of this change. I suppose I had to make an unaccustomed physical effort in order for the benefits of the treatment to become apparent. I haven't had any further dizzy spells or queasiness; all the undesirable side effects turned out to be short-lived.

I could easily have carried Ève upstairs in my arms like a bride. But I set her back on her feet and we climbed the stairs together, hand in hand. It was early afternoon, and the upstairs bedroom was flooded with winter light. The sheets were the color of the dunes, and the pillowcases smelled of cut grass.

I never imagined when I went round to my neighbor that our conversation would take such a turn. Clearly, we've both been craving intimacy. We wrapped ourselves around each other like we'd clinked glasses earlier, to banish our unnamable fears while pretending to celebrate our victories. In this sense we are both, she and I, undeniably hypocritical; but it's a legitimate hypocrisy, quite commendable really, given that its sole aim was to banish perfectly good reasons to die.

As it has been every time with Ève, the sex was alternately playful, mischievous, tender, sardonic, subtle, and fiery. With her, intelligence doesn't fall asleep when sensuality is awakened.

But enough of the oblique compliments. Suffice it to say I would have stayed with her all night if my goddaughter hadn't been waiting for me alone back at home. Eventually I forced myself to get up, get dressed, and leave, and it was a wrench.

*

When I arrived home Adrienne was still up and we talked until dawn about the people of Empedocles and the strange adventure we've been on since they came into our lives.

My opinion on them varies, as must be clear in this journal, which by its very nature privileges candor over coherence. Sometimes I miss the Before Times, when our civilization seemed like the apotheosis of Creation, and sometimes I'm thrilled to be experiencing such an epochal and potentially productive upheaval.

I kept emphasizing that last point during my conversation with Adrienne. I don't want her to harbor resentment towards these people at the very moment she's hoping to start working with them—if they return, I should add, given that as I'm writing this they still haven't, and the radio waves remain unnervingly silent.

Monday, November 29th

It's been thirty-six hours now since they left. I keep thinking they aren't going to come back, that I should start trying to draw up a preliminary assessment of our brief encounter with them. But then every time I think that I change my mind, precisely because of the blackout—phone, radio, screen, everything. I can't help thinking that if they keep punishing us like this it's because they haven't yet decided to leave for good.

This morning at low tide several dozen islanders crossed the Gouay to Antioch and spent the day pacing up and down the beach. They complained and consoled each other, all the while keeping watch on the horizon. At sunset they left, too miserable to speak. I don't know what's going on elsewhere in the world, but I assume that wherever the ships from Empedocles cast anchor there are thousands of men and women, waiting for them and weeping like orphans.

Here on the archipelago, we have other things to worry about. A trawler has been lost at sea. It headed out at daybreak to an area called Rochebelle, whose waters are supposed to be teeming with fish. It was meant to return at nightfall, but there's no sign of it. As I write, there's no means of communicating with the boat and the crew hasn't sent out a distress signal. The crew on board, three brothers and one of their sons, are experienced and sober professionals. The sea has been exceptionally calm all day, so the islanders are convinced that the boat must have been boarded by the ferryman's compatriots.

I have noticed that they are now considered in the eyes of the local people as both saviors and predators. They have colonized our imagination, giving substance no less to our ancestral fears than to our hopes. I've blessed them as much as I've cursed them, and I imagine I'll continue to vacillate.

In terms of blessing them, I'm grateful they spared us from a devastating conflict and offered us a sort of safety net to put right both our past recklessness and our future actions. I'm also far from unmoved by the treatment they gave me; if they do return, I'm sure I'll often make use of their medical science in the future. For this alone, I can only feel gratitude and respect for them.

But when it comes to cursing them, things are less cut and dried; it's not nearly as easy to argue the case. What makes me most angry with our so-called saviors is the way they've reduced our entire history, with its proud cohort of heroes, conquerors, saints, and discoverers, to a minor episode of the past, in the blink of an eye reducing my people, all people, to the rank of natives. Not that we've had many scruples when it comes to doing the same thing to other cultures. And I wouldn't dream of suggesting that the humiliation inflicted on us by our guardians is undeserved.

Here I am again, saying things that Ève wouldn't disagree with. Generally, I think I'm more nuanced than her, less provocative, and not in the least misanthropic. But having spent the last few hours mulling things over, I realize our civilization has just undergone the same ordeal that we have perpetrated on others throughout our history, right up to the present day.

Since my eyes first opened, I've witnessed two phenomena that today, on this day of rest, are becoming clearer. Firstly, the decisive triumph of a nation which, in the last few decades, has emerged as the only superpower, and arguably the only civilization—obviously I'm talking about the United States of America. And now, the quite unexpected triumph of the nation of Empedocles, which no one was prepared for.

I've just remembered something Moro mentioned a few days ago that I forgot to write about here. It clearly has a certain resonance, since it's appeared lately on several Latin American websites. "*Ahora los yanquis tienen sus propios yanquis,*" which translates roughly as "Now the Yankees have their own Yankees."

As a rule, before any civilization finds itself definitively downgraded, it will have already gone through a lengthy period of decline, often centuries-long, and will have had time to adjust to its marginalization and accept its increasing insignificance. Sudden, unanticipated societal collapse, such as occurred at the time of the conquistadors, remains the exception. I've referred to that period of history more than once because today's turmoil keeps bringing it to mind. What the Aztecs and the Incas experienced is the same as what's taking place before our very eyes: the entirely unforeseen devaluation of our knowledge, our vision of the world, our identity, our dignity.

All the cards of universal human history have been reshuffled and must now be redistributed.

Whether our guardians decide to stay or to leave, the cards will certainly not be dealt out the same way as before.

*

I invited Ève over for dinner this evening to meet Adrienne. I prepared some soup with fish I had in the freezer. I'm hoping that the fishing picks up again soon, or the people of the archipelago— beginning with us on Antioch—will soon run out of everything. No food is being delivered from the mainland, it isn't harvest season, and it's beginning to remind the older islanders of the food shortages of the past. But I have a hundred and six bottles in my cellar; at least I'll have wine for a while.

When I introduced Ève to Adrienne, I heard myself say, "She's my sweetheart!" We all burst out laughing, and then I added in the same register, "We share the island. Her domain is to the north, mine is to the south. She writes, I draw, sometimes we argue, and then we drink to the health of the friends of Empedocles."

"That's in a manner of speaking," said Ève. "As far as their health goes, they hardly need our good wishes. What usually happens is I drink to the decline of men, and your godfather joins me out of politeness. Then we go to bed together as a way of reconciling ourselves to the human condition."

I blushed. The two women were gently teasing me. I don't think I'll ever get used to the candor with which people talk about such things nowadays. But as the evening went on, with the help of the wine, the three of us talked with such directness and honesty, without any drama or prudishness, as though it were our last night together before the world ended.

I don't think I've ever enjoyed such a heartfelt, honest, intense evening in my whole life. Which makes me even less willing to discuss it here. I'd feel like I was breaking the charm.

Tuesday, November 30ᵗʰ

I got up this morning and wandered down to the La Roche-aux-Fras beach to see what was going on, keeping an eye out towards the horizon. I knew I probably wouldn't see the Empedocles ship, and indeed I didn't.

Yesterday I was still taken by the absurd idea that the punishment they're inflicting on us means they are still interested in us. Today I can only smile at my naivety and blindness. All the evidence suggests that the sole purpose of the communications blackout is to provide them with cover while they make their way back to the country they came from without being pursued.

Last night Ève and Adrienne seemed convinced our guardians won't stay away for long. They tried their utmost to persuade me, as though if I came round to their way of thinking it would increase the probability of things coming to pass as they hoped. Wearily, I told them they were probably right.

They have both been profoundly affected by what has happened, though for different reasons.

Ève says it's as though she has woken up with a start from the most beautiful dream. "What's been going on for the last three weeks is what I've been praying for since I was a child, without daring to believe it might happen: that a power would appear from out of the blue, declare men to be incompetent and place them under its control; take away their bombs, missiles, military bases, their palaces and prisons, their useless gadgets, their laboratories and abattoirs … And then, quite without warning, when I was at absolute rock bottom, my dream came true!" She is still in a state of euphoria, but I suspect she'll fall back into despair and depression if our saviors don't return.

My goddaughter's conviction that they will come back is motivated by something else: scientific curiosity. She's always been fascinated by advances in medical knowledge. To her, "the friends of Empedocles" are peerless geniuses who have made the kinds of miraculous leaps of progress that we can only dream of. She wants to study with them and try to understand how they have attained such heights.

"Pausanias has promised to teach me their medicine. I'm sure he will if it's possible, and I hope I'll be up to it. Anyway, I'm going to study as hard as I can, even if it takes me the whole of the rest of my life."

The three of us were sitting in my living room drinking Japanese green tea. The sun was low in the sky, but it was still bright enough outside that there was no need to light candles. The ocean had a rosy luster. It was shimmering and empty. Not a single boat to be seen.

Ève asked Adrienne if she had tried the healing tunnel.

"I wanted to. But there were always actual sick people waiting in line. I'm in perfectly good health."

"Didn't that handsome young doctor suggest it?"

Adrienne smiled. "He did. He tried to get me to go in it last night. But it was late, I was a bit drunk, and there were dozens of people still lined up outside. I promised I'd be there today without fail."

"Did he kiss you?"

I started in surprise. Not my goddaughter though. She seemed to think it was a perfectly reasonable question.

"No, he didn't. We just talked. I asked him the thing that's been really bugging me: how come their scientific knowledge is so far ahead of ours? He didn't directly answer the question. But what he said helped me understand.

"He explained that we tend to associate scientific discoveries with specific eras. So, for example, the law of universal gravitation was *discovered* in the seventeenth century; it wasn't *born* in Newton's time, it was just that it was discovered at that particular moment, because that was when the progress made by scientists in terms of understanding the phenomenon reached maturity. The laws of nature have obviously been the same since the dawn of time; the law of gravity could have been discovered at any point in the last thousand or two thousand years. It's the same in all disciplines.

"And what this means is that when people are allowed to follow their own path without their minds being hampered by taboos and prejudices, when all that matters is beating back ignorance, they make far more progress than everyone else, who find themselves left far behind. According to Pausanias, that explains the ancient Greek miracle, and it also explains why his people are so far ahead of us."

"And how did they manage to survive for centuries?" I asked. "Stay out of sight, safe from persecution? Keep going on their own path?"

"The sea," said Ève, staring through the window

at the horizon. "Ever since Agamemnon told us about his ancestors' journey, I've been wondering the same thing: how did they manage to protect themselves? How did they keep the flame of the ancient miracle burning? By staying on the run? Hiding in caves? No. The answer's much simpler and more logical, and one day it just came to me out of the blue: the ocean, of course. Isn't it the largest country of all, with the fewest frontiers, the least governed and regulated through history? And isn't it true that there have always been coastal zones where peoples have lived without being in thrall to any authority or empire?"

"If he ever does come back, I'm going to torture the ferryman until he tells us the truth," I said laughing.

"They'll all be back," declared my neighbor. "I don't doubt it for a second."

"I hope God hears you," said Adrienne.

I didn't say anything. For the time being, all our questions and prayers are justified. I'm going to stick to giving an account of them, without attempting to provide answers or argue for any side.

*

One more thing before I stop writing for today: the trawler that lost contact yesterday returned to Port-Atlantique this evening with only half its crew. When they set out there were four men on board, three brothers plus one of their sons. Two of the brothers fell overboard. Only the father and son survived. What happened? An accident? A fight? A settling of scores? The two survivors swear the other men were swept overboard by a huge wave.

I don't know whether to believe them. The only thing that seems certain is that the friends of Empedocles played no role in the drama, neither as shipwreckers nor rescuers. Which only reinforces the feeling I have that the parenthesis that opened in our lives is now closing, and we ought perhaps to relinquish our habit of seeing them as the source of all our fortunes and misfortunes.

Of course, it's possible I'm completely wrong. That's definitely what Ève and Adrienne would say if I had the temerity to tell them what I thought.

I now know why they sailed away from the coast and why we are being punished.

It's because of the bombing. It took place on Saturday, at 5.40 p.m. Eastern Standard Time. It was twenty to midnight here, long after our dinner was over. Adrienne had just come in from walking Pausanias back to the ship.

But because of the communications blackout we've only just heard the news.

It happened in the place where President Milton was treated, on the Washington Channel, south-west of the capital. A massive explosion destroyed the hospital ship, killing physicians, patients undergoing treatment, people waiting in line, police officers standing guard, and some random passersby who had the bad luck to be in the vicinity.

At last count eighty-eight people were killed, nine of whom worked on the hospital ship, and over two hundred and fifty were wounded.

The explosive device seems to have been put on a boat that approached the floating hospital under some pretext or other. But there are lots of theories circulating this morning online, talk of missiles, lethal drones, and suicide bombers.

There's every reason to believe that our so-called protectors were caught completely off guard by the attack. So far they haven't attempted to salvage either the wreck or the corpses of their people—not that there's much to salvage, by all accounts. Their immediate reaction was to cut all communication and make a getaway. In the minutes after the explosion all their vessels, all over the world, had weighed anchor and sailed to international waters.

Due to the imposed blackout, few people heard about what had happened in the immediate aftermath. News of the attack spread by word of mouth around Washington, and by evening leaflets were being handed out in the vicinity of the Capitol and the White House by an organization—called, rather perniciously, "The New Founding Fathers"—claiming responsibility for the attack. The text read:

> *For eighteen days the territory of the United States has been subjected to an unprecedented threat to our independence, our sovereignty, and the liberty and dignity of all our citizens.*
>
> *A gang of pirates and merchants of illusions is shamelessly blackmailing our leaders, who have not had the courage to stand up to them and have gone so far as to order our troops to passively submit to their demands.*
>
> *The greatest military force in the world will not allow itself to be disarmed!*
>
> *The most powerful and prosperous nation on God's earth will not allow itself to be humiliated!*
>
> *We pledge to fight, with all our might, by all means, and at any cost, to prove ourselves worthy of the freedom our forefathers bequeathed us.*
>
> *God bless the United States of America!*

Although whoever was behind the declaration didn't explicitly claim responsibility for the attack, the signature hints at it in a subtle and slightly odd way:

The New Founding Fathers
Washington Channel
Thursday 5:40 P.M.

Contemptuous of the people of Empedocles, describing them not as a "nation" or an "intervening power" but a "gang of pirates" practicing blackmail and trickery, the text doesn't let US officials off the hook either, starting with the president. Even though he is not named, the very fact that the attack took place in the Washington Channel and directly targeted the people who treated him sends a pointed message.

Milton, to my knowledge, has yet to respond. The only official reaction has been a statement condemning the loss of life and the blind use of violence. Though it came from the White House it didn't name the head of state—most unusual, particularly for a tragedy on this scale. It makes one wonder if it came from the incumbent or the acting president. There seems to be some uncertainty around this question. The media is still calling Boulder the acting president. Evidently Milton has neither resumed his duties nor resigned. I am guessing there's some scheming going on behind the scenes. The only person who could enlighten me is of course Moro, but I haven't been able to get hold of him, which puzzles and worries me. I've left him two voicemails and sent an email but have heard nothing in response.

He must be up to his eyeballs, especially if a diplomatic game is being played at the highest ranks of the administration. But this silence isn't like him at all. Even when he's incredibly busy, he takes the time to send a brief reply to his closest friends. *I'll be in touch*, or something similar.

I hope he didn't decide to go for treatment on the floating hospital at the wrong moment.

No, that wouldn't have been like him either. Not at all.

Thursday, December 2nd

I was right to be concerned about my friend. He'd been held against his will for five days and nights and it was only today that he was released.

What happened to him is emblematic of the bitter standoff in Washington that's playing out partly in public and partly in the shadows, the outcome of which remains as yet unknown.

Moro's troubles began last Saturday morning, several hours before the bombing. He'd just received a desperate call from first lady Cynthia Milton, telling him her husband was planning to resign that day, and hoping that his closest advisor and friend would use his influence to persuade him to change his mind.

Clearly Moro was unsurprised by the turn of events, as he made clear to me this morning during a long phone call.

"Howard had gotten it into his head that he was going to have to step down as president the moment he agreed to be treated by the doctors from Empedocles," he told me. "First off, as I think I told you, before the operation he decided to notify officially the speaker of the House of Representatives and the president of the Senate of his temporary state of incapacity, despite the fact he was not obliged to so by the Constitution; then after it he failed to resume his duties. Whenever one of his close advisors tried to talk to him about it, he said he needed time to think and to make sure the treatment he'd received hadn't triggered any physical or mental problems.

"All this was obviously motivated by a sense of guilt, because he felt he was in some sense collaborating with the occupiers after he'd accepted their promise to cure him. But alongside his ethical concerns, there's always some subtle political calculation going on. Namely, he wants to present his experience on the hospital ship as a risky undertaking requiring a dose of bravery and dedication, rather than a privilege granted to him by 'those people.' He reckons that if the American people see it the same way, he'll be able to maintain his moral integrity and legitimacy. He keeps telling everyone around him he feels sick and dizzy and his vision is blurred.

"I get it, I really do. Of course, I'd strongly advised him not to declare himself in a state of incapacity in the first place, then I'd begged him to resume his duties immediately after. But deep down I have to admit his little game isn't entirely pointless, if it makes him feel better and dissuades him from stepping down.

"But then Dr. Abel made his statement, and that made things a lot worse. With his dramatic announcement that the president was cured, the doctor had him backed into a corner. Not intentionally, of course. If Abel had ever imagined his statement would have such grave political implications, he'd have consulted his patient before making it. But he was obsessed, and I understand this, by the scientific aspect. He's discovered the medicine he's devoted his whole life to is worthless now. Nothing else matters to him.

"So basically, Howard felt obliged to react to the public announcement about his recovery. And now the whole nation is going to demand to be treated by these physicians, and he can't cope with the pressure. How can he deprive sick Americans of the life-saving treatment he's benefited from? For a head of state that would be simply unforgivable—didn't Alexander the Great pour away the water a soldier brought him because he didn't want to be the only one of his army to slake his thirst? Yet, on the other hand, Milton can't allow the people of Empedocles to remain among us indefinitely without looking like a traitor, or at least a sellout. He's completely demoralized by this dilemma, convinced the only honorable solution for him is to give up power.

"So anyway, Cynthia called me on Saturday. She passed me on to Howard. I begged him to delay his resignation for one more hour, so we could speak face-to-face. He agreed, out of consideration for thirty years of friendship. I left my apartment straightaway. Three men were waiting for me outside the building. They flashed their badges, took my cellphone, which I was holding in my hand, and told me to follow them. They led me down into a basement where they pretended to interrogate me. Really, all they wanted to do was detain me. Maybe they thought that when the president realized I wasn't coming he'd sign his letter of resignation without bothering to wait. But that's not what happened. Seeing I hadn't come, and I wasn't answering my cellphone, he realized something was up. He put the letter away in a drawer and decided to wait until things seemed a little clearer."

"Who were these people?"

"Patriots."

"Oh, is that what you call them! You really are not at all a bitter person, are you?"

"I don't want to let myself be so blinded by my own bad luck that I can't see the bigger picture. What's been going on for the last three weeks is seen by many Americans as a threat to their nation, its sovereignty, its status as a superpower. They think Howard's been too soft on defending the interests of the nation, and he needs to be gotten rid of. And since I was on my way to see him with the specific purpose of persuading him to remain in his post, I was considered an obstacle, so I had to be, as it were, taken out of circulation."

"You're being very good-humored about it."

"Only because I'm free again. I wasn't nearly so good-humored while I was being held. I showered them with insults."

"Do you think it's the same people who carried out the bombing?"

"I don't know if it's the same organization, but they definitely share the same beliefs and mindset. From their point of view, the people of Empedocles needed to experience a shock, to really suffer, some of them had to be killed, so that they would decide to leave. For a civilization so proud of being able to extend life indefinitely, to be torn apart by a bomb is simply unendurable. It turned out to be an impressively successful strategy. As soon as their people were killed, they left.

"Of course, there were American victims too. But we're used to that, sadly. We can write it off. They, apparently, cannot. That's their weakness, and their enemies know it."

As my friend was talking, it occurred to me that the difference in the ability to absorb loss is usually seen as a weakness and a liability for westerners in relation to less advanced societies. But face-to-face with the people of Empedocles, it's as if the mirror has been reversed. Moro is clearly aware of this too, it's something we've already talked about it. But I didn't remind him now. I didn't want to get into it. Today I wanted him to tell me about what he'd been through.

"You've explained why they held you, and it sounds plausible. But why did they keep you for five days?"

"There are a few possible explanations. The first is that the kidnappers were afraid of being followed. They'd acted in haste. Someone must have been listening in on my conversation with Cynthia and Howard and then given the order to stop me getting to the White House. They weren't masked, and I know exactly how to get to the building they took me to. When the bombing took place a few hours later they must have realized that if they let me go immediately investigators would have no trouble figuring out their involvement. Since they didn't want to kill me, they held on to me while awaiting further instructions."

"And what made them release you today?"

"Because there won't be an investigation of the bombing. Sure, they'll make it look like there has been, they'll say the guilty will be found and punished, but it'll be covered up in the end."

I was astonished that he was speaking so candidly about something so serious, especially now he knows his phone is tapped. Then it occurred to me he knew exactly what he was doing. If these so-called Patriots were listening in, they'd hear the message he wanted them to hear. That there's no need for them worry, they have nothing to fear if Milton remains president.

It was clear from what Moro told me, though he didn't say so in as many words, that the bombing of the floating hospital was not the work of a handful of extremists, but an operation carried out by the very people responsible for protecting the country: the armed forces or one of the security agencies, or a coalition of several different bodies. The prevailing impression of late in every branch of the federal government has been that something must be done, by whatever means, to drive out those who, in one of our earlier conversations, my friend euphemistically called "the uninvited."

Would last Saturday's deadly explosion be enough to realize this objective? It can't be ruled out, but it's too early to say. Nothing suggests at this stage that they are ready to accept their defeat, swallow their pride, give up their plans, and definitively abandon their projects and their involvement in our world.

It would take the insight of an ostrich to believe that just because we can no longer see our guardians, our guardians can no longer see us. And are no longer watching and waiting in the shadows to intervene once more if and when they deem it necessary.

Saturday, December 4th

I didn't write a single page in this journal yesterday. I went through it, corrected spelling mistakes, checked the sources of various quotations I'd highlighted. Then I slipped the first three notebooks into a grey folder provisionally labeled *Evidence*. The fourth, the one I'm writing in now, which is only a third full, I thought I'd conclude over the next few days with an epilogue a few paragraphs long, before putting it in the folder and never touching it again.

Not that the story is over—I suspect it's going to go on for a while, in various configurations, and won't ever definitively come to an end; but the role of eyewitness I've taken on over the last few weeks is no longer really needed since the hasty departure of our uninvited brothers.

My sudden change of mind has come about because Saturday's unrest makes me think that the events I've recounted in these pages remain current, not simply an episode of history, and that my daily observations, for the time being at least, still have a purpose.

I'm thinking in particular of the ongoing tug-of-war in Washington, which is now taking on the contours of a Greek tragedy and will likely have major global repercussions.

This morning when I woke up, the international media were reporting what was said last night by acting president Gary Boulder. I didn't catch it live because of the time difference.

It wasn't an official statement broadcast from the Oval Office. It would have been clumsy of Boulder to have adopted such an unmistakably presidential stance. He chose instead to express himself during a lengthy televised interview, but his words still smacked of an attempted power grab.

When the journalist Kate Stormfield asked him what he'd thought when President Milton had agreed to be treated by the doctors from Empedocles, his words were those of an assassin, manifestly prepared in advance and accompanied by a wince of fake sorrow.

"Howard has always been an honest and honorable man. I thought he had just had a moment of weakness and distraction. He gave in, as you know, to pressure from those around him, and I am sure he regretted it straightaway, and that he's agonized over it ever since. I still have the greatest respect and affection for him, but I think in this case he showed a lack of judgement. He allowed personal considerations to take precedence over the best interests of the nation."

"But don't you think it's natural to do anything and everything one can to cure terminal cancer?" asked the journalist.

"Of course it's natural to want to be cured. What is not natural, however, is to imagine that man can ever triumph over death. This is, if I may be so bold, an illusion that has spread widely in recent weeks. An insane and sinful illusion. God alone is master of life and death, and when a mortal, whoever he may be, poor or rich, lowly or powerful, arrogantly believes he can take this decision out of the hands of the Creator and into his own, he is committing a sin for which he is bound to be punished."

"Listening to you, I guess you weren't upset when the floating hospitals of Empedocles left our shores."

"You guess right, Kate. Any bargain with these people seemed to me, from the very beginning, to be a pact with the devil. Fortunately, our great nation soon reasserted itself. Where we might have opted for submission, capitulation, and empty promises, instead we chose resistance, we rejected the sinful option, and that's something we can be proud of."

Questioned about Saturday's explosion, Boulder carefully avoided condemning the perpetrators, contenting himself merely with regretting "the loss of so many innocent American lives," and expressing the hope that they "had not died in vain."

I called Moro as soon as I could to hear his reaction. He was appalled.

"What an appalling thing to say! A leader who fails to condemn the bombing, approves of its objectives, welcomes its consequences, can you imagine? A high official simply must maintain a modicum of decency, regardless of his political position, his ambition, his frustration."

It wasn't just Boulder my friend was furious with.

"None of this would have happened if Howard hadn't been such a fool. He should never have declared himself in a state of incapacity, and he should *never* have allowed Gary to go to sleep and wake up as president of the United States."

"But, as I understand it, all Milton needs to do is send a letter, and he can resume his duties and end this bizarre situation, right?"

"In principle, yes, that's right. And Howard did eventually send the damned letter last night. But Boulder immediately wrote back, and now he's sent a letter to the speaker of the House of Representatives and the president of the Senate challenging the president's decision."

"On what basis?"

"He's claiming that the reasons the president was officially considered to be in a state of incapacity remain valid, and therefore he must not be allowed to take up his duties again."

"Is that even legal?"

"Wait, there's worse: from the moment the president's decision is contested, the vice president is the one who holds power."

"How is that possible?"

"Yes, it's crazy, but I've read and reread the twenty-fifth amendment, the text is a bit muddled, but it seems to indicate that when the president's decision is contested by the vice president, it's the vice president who continues to govern."

"Up until what point?"

"Up until Congress settles the decision, which can take three weeks. I can't imagine what the legislators had in mind when they drafted the amendment. I imagine their main concern was to avoid the president's chair remaining empty. Whatever it was, they can't have anticipated a situation like this."

"And now?"

Moro's evasive response made it clear he didn't want to tell me over the phone the options he was considering, for fear of divulging his strategy to his opponents. I suppose there must be various judicial solutions. At this level, it's a very tightly fought game of chess.

But the power struggle is also being played out in the media, and the route chosen today by Milton's supporters was to respond to the vice president's interview with another televised interview, this time with the first lady, who is indisputably the most popular public figure in America today.

The hour-long program broke all audience records. Cynthia Milton set out from the beginning to demolish Boulder. Her aim was to utterly discredit him, without once mentioning his name or status.

"Yesterday I heard some foolish and terrible things said, unworthy of our great nation. It seems that if someone you love is sick with cancer or Alzheimer's disease, and your greatest hope is for them to be cured, you are committing a sin. It seems that if your parent or your spouse or your child is seriously ill, or in an accident, and you would do anything to save their life, you are defying the Creator.

"Such careless words are counter to all common sense, human decency, and our God-given laws. Let me tell you with confidence and conviction: it is a sin to believe that God is no more than the purveyor of sickness and the guardian of death, and that the very act of choosing life sets you against Him and offends Him.

"The worst sin is to believe that God rejoices in our physical and mental suffering and feels diminished when those we love escape death.

"In the olden days half of women died in childbirth, and half of babies died in infancy. Who was responsible for these deaths? God, or the ignorance of men? I say ignorance kills, and progress saves. Those who believe that God is the enemy of progress and the ally of ignorance, they are the sinners, in my eyes. They have nothing to do with God or religion, or the pioneering spirit of our great nation.

"I have also heard accusations of arrogance. But is there anything more arrogant than a man purporting to decide for us that those we love must remain sick and die? Anyone who professes such ambition belongs to different era, and certainly should not be at the head of a country as advanced and free as ours.

"Surely it is up to us to decide if we want our loved ones to be cured. And I say *yes, we do want it, with every fiber of our beings, and we will shout it from the rooftops!* We will say it however and wherever we can, on television, on the radio, on social media, in public. Let no one forbid us from treating and saving the lives of our spouses, our children, our parents. We will do all we can to sustain their physical and mental health, for as long as we can. Nothing matters so much; no objective could be more noble. And because fate has introduced us to these people, with their extraordinary medical knowledge, we now have recourse to their science, for us to benefit from without hesitation or shame. Let us welcome them into our midst!

"What our nation needs today is not a power struggle or an ideological debate. We need a wake-up call, to save our loved ones' lives. I fought for the man I love to be treated, and thanks to you he has been cured. I am proud of that. I would go so far as to say it is the most beautiful thing I have done in my entire life. You helped me win this fight and win it I did. A week ago, Howard had not long to live, and today he is in excellent health.

"The fight is yours now. Yes, every one of you, man or woman, young or old: it is up to you to fight to save your own lives and the lives of those you love, to eradicate sickness and push back death.

"It is the most beautiful, noble, and honorable struggle there is, and one which I will continue to wage with everything I have. I hope that all those who hear me, all those who hope to save the lives of their loved ones, will have the confidence to join me, and I am sure that our prayers will be answered."

The First Lady's words didn't exactly lack demagoguery, it has to be said. But if her aim was to touch her audience, she succeeded magnificently.

Thinking back to the impassioned reaction to her earlier initiative ten days ago, I'm sure that many Americans, women especially, are going to be sympathetic to this latest appeal and will give her their full support.

Sunday, December 5ᵗʰ

I lacked vision last night.

Of course, I knew that Cynthia Milton's emotional and combative words would have an impact. But I'd missed the main point—the great fury that has been smoldering all over the world and has been unleashed today. Fury against what? Against the usurping American politician who uttered such indecent words? Against the deadly attack that destroyed the floating hospital and persuaded the doctors of Empedocles to leave? Against all those who take it upon themselves to make decisions on our behalf, about this life and beyond? Not only, according to Ève. She said things that trouble, even anger me. But the more I think about it the more I realize she has a point.

This morning I felt like I was watching a replay of the scene from last week when, immediately after the First Lady's call to arms, Americans went out into the streets to demonstrate their support. Once again, hordes of protestors flocked to iconic sites like Times Square in New York, where hundreds of people had already gathered to watch the interview on giant screens, and then in other cities: Boston, Washington, Chicago, Miami, San Francisco, Baltimore. It was as though history were repeating itself after a ten-day interval.

But it only seemed that way. In the interim something fundamental has changed. It wasn't easy to see as long as the events taking place didn't reveal it; it was only this evening that I realized, and it will take me much longer to gauge the full consequences.

The thing I've only just figured out is that the arrival of the friends of Empedocles, with their advanced knowledge of medicine and their floating hospitals, has led to an upending of priorities and values the world over. Now that it's possible to conquer disease, ward off old age, postpone death—all without spending a cent, thanks to what can only be called a gift from heaven, or rather the sea—no aspect of human life has the same importance it used to, whether it's money, time, work, social hierarchies, or power struggles. Everything that has governed human interaction up till now is becoming marginal, anachronistic, superfluous.

Since last night, images of what's going on in public places across America have been broadcast without a break on multiple online sites. I watched them for hours, taking notes.

My first observation is that people are demonstrating not only in countries where free expression has always been the norm, but also in countries where those who dare to take to the streets are brave, even suicidal. It seems the desire for good health is so strong that fear of the police no longer has any effect. And it turns out that even national leaders have such mixed feelings about it they're no longer trying to impose their authority. Even with all the privileges and prerogatives they have to protect, the powerful of this world—kings and queens, presidents, prime ministers, marshals, military governors—can't forget that they are first and foremost human beings who will one day fall ill like anyone else, and obtaining the right for them and those close to them to be treated on the floating hospitals matters more to them than all the privileges bestowed by rank and power. Consequently the demonstrators, even those who are their political opponents, have in a way become their allies. Which presumably explains why no one anywhere in the world is cracking down on the vast rallies taking place under their noses.

The makeup of these crowds is also atypical. There are as many old people as young, many more women than men. Parents holding their children's hands and carrying infants. Visibly sick people with mobile drips marching alongside those who are fighting fit. People of all origins and social classes have taken over public spaces—at the last count thirty million people in three thousand cities in forty countries have settled down in streets and squares, on blankets, crates, and folding chairs, sitting there night and day, in rain and shine and snow, holding placards, filming the crowds on the cellphones they wave above their heads, chanting slogans: "Bring back the hospitals!" "Bring back the doctors!" or simply, "Bring 'em back!"

The whole world has its eyes glued to these crowds. Nothing else is happening, anywhere. No one is travelling or working, everything is on hold. No one's talking about anything else, at home, in the circles of power, in the media, or on social networks. A strange revolution is taking place, the most extensive, peaceable, irrepressible revolution that has ever been.

To hear Ève, what we're seeing unfold is nothing less than the death throes of the old world, of the world as we used to know it. Its demise seems so inevitable that she speaks about it as if it has already happened.

"Future historians will say our civilization was so worm-eaten that it took only a flick of the wrist for the whole edifice to collapse. The final blow came from an unexpected direction, but it was inevitable it would come along sooner or later. We invented lethal weapons that were bound to turn against us eventually. You know, some diabolical device, nuclear, bacteriological, or chemical, could have exploded tonight in a major city, killing tens of thousands of people and sparking global panic. With a little luck, we might have delayed the disaster another year or two or five. But could we have avoided it indefinitely? Surely not. Hatreds are on the rise, and technology, sometimes knowingly, sometimes quite innocently, has created tools for them to be unleashed and destroy everything. What chance do we have of escaping disaster? None. Which is why our contemporaries have clung like this to their unexpected saviors."

"Do you really think all these demonstrators have come to the same conclusion as you?" I asked.

"They might not use the same words, but they all think it. It's the same calamitous reality and fear everywhere."

I pursed my lips doubtfully by way of reply. I can never tell if my novelist neighbor sees things with complete clarity or if she's mistaken. It's certainly true she has a tendency to get carried away, but I've learned never to make light of her insights.

*

Another significant difference between the protests of ten days ago and those of today is that the earlier ones were essentially in support of a woman fighting her husband's obduracy. No doubt the demonstrators were thinking of all the sick people they knew, of the beneficial impact it would have for them if Cynthia Milton were successful and set a precedent; but the mobilization was first and foremost in support of her, simply because they were moved by her predicament. This time it's for themselves and their loved ones that people have come out into the streets. All with the same demand, wherever and whoever they are: the return of the floating hospitals.

The First Lady is well aware of this. In a second interview broadcast this evening on giant screens to crowds of people from Tiananmen to Times Square, she made an appeal that exactly corresponds to what the demonstrators want:

"I would like to address a personal message to a man I met a fortnight ago, whom I hold in the greatest esteem: Mr. Demosthenes."

She said his name again, louder this time: "Mr. Demosthenes!" She stopped and waited, as if she had literally called out his name and was waiting to hear his reply. The demonstrators respected her dramatic words with a brief but reverential silence. Then she spoke again, directly addressing him:

"I do not know your role in your nation's leadership, but I met with you when you came as an emissary to negotiate with the US government. You stayed overnight at the White House, and the next day you thanked me for the gracious welcome you received.

"On that occasion, you promised to do what you could to treat Howard, who was suffering from terminal lung cancer. You kept your promise. Today, thanks to you, my husband is well again. His physician, Dr. Abel, attests to this. As I have not seen you since, and I do not know where to write you, I have not been able to express my gratitude to you. So I would like to take this opportunity to thank you publicly, and equally to thank all the staff on the hospital ship where he was treated.

"You've given Howard back his life. Your friends have given us back our lives—and in return we have given them death. Immoral, misguided fanatics chose to kill the very people who treated the president. I promised myself I would thank every single person involved in treating Howard, and instead I find myself offering my condolences to their loved ones.

"The criminal hand that murdered your citizens and ours, that in a single moment murdered those devoted to healing and those desperate to be healed, this hand wants to keep us apart, to send you away from us. And yet, quite unintentionally, it has mingled our blood with yours, mingled your fate with ours. From now on we are united, and we shall remain so, for better or for worse. For better, I hope—for life and for progress. We shall remain united, all of us, brothers and sisters of all ages and all origins.

"My dear friend Demosthenes, please know that you are always welcome in our home. Howard and I will always be grateful to you and happy to see you. Come back! Come back with your friends and your nation's wonderful physicians!

"I know I speak on behalf of all those listening, all those people filling the streets the world over, when I say: Come back! You will always be welcome here!"

The standoff in Washington ended suddenly and unexpectedly in favor of President Milton.

I don't know if his wife's address had anything to do with it, but the massive demonstrations certainly played a role. The vice president threw in the towel during the night, with what pretty much amounted to an apology for having claimed that Milton was unable to discharge his duties.

According to the various analysts I heard on the radio this morning when I woke up, Boulder only withdrew to avoid an even more mortifying defeat. Congress was due to vote today, likely unanimously, for the reinstatement of Milton to his full duties as president. Boulder, about to be so fiercely humiliated that he probably wouldn't have been able to hold on to the vice presidency, acted first to save his neck.

American public opinion is so massively behind the president that his political opponents must keep a low profile now, praying to heaven that the people of Empedocles are so traumatized by the deadly attack that they themselves make the choice not to reappear.

It's possible that things will soon become much clearer. In a statement, a White House spokesperson announced that a ceremony will be held midday on Wednesday at the Arlington Military Cemetery in honor of the victims of the bombing. At the last count 123 people were killed in the attack, ninety-two Americans and thirty-one foreign nationals, nine of whom were working on the floating hospital.

The statement also included an invitation to the leaders of countries whose citizens were victims of the bombing. Departing from the text he was reading, the spokesperson said that the president very much hoped that representatives of "the nation of Empedocles" would respond positively to the invitation. "They will be warmly welcomed both by the administration and the people of the United States, and the leader of their delegation will be invited to speak at the ceremony."

So there it is. An appointment, in public at a specific time, where the eyes of the world will be turned upon them.

Apart from a tiny minority, which I am lucky enough to be part of, most people have never set eyes on any of these men and women. Their curiosity will be intense.

Will they come? If they do, how many will join the delegation? What does their leader look like? What will he say on the podium?

All over the world people will be asking these same questions and a thousand more, right up until the appointed time.

*

This afternoon, to pass the time, I tried calling Agamemnon on his cellphone. It was, almost literally, as pointless as drawing a knife through water.

I heard a click and then the familiar recorded message. It wasn't much, but I'd have been a great deal more disappointed if an automated voice had told me the number no longer existed. I began to leave a message—"I was just calling to find out if I'll be seeing you anytime soon"—and was wondering how to go on, when in came Adrienne and Ève, back from a hike. Without thinking, I ended the message, "Ève and Adrienne send their love," and hung up.

"Who was that?" they said in unison. "The ferryman," I said, to surprise them. Their eyes widened.

"Where is he?"

I paused for a moment before admitting I'd simply left a message.

"I just wanted to tell him we're looking forward to seeing him."

The two women would have been well within their rights to laugh at me. But neither of them said a word. Instead they each came up and gave me an appreciative kiss on the cheek.

I'd imagined the day before the Arlington ceremony as one of waiting and contemplation. But, as fate would have it, it would impact my life in a quite different way. I'm still stunned, and I suspect I will be for some time to come.

Lists of the many world leaders who will be attending the ceremony alongside President Milton are being regularly updated in the media. Some are coming to pay their respects to their own citizens who died in the attack, but most are coming out of sheer curiosity, to see the Empedocles envoys up close, and shake their hands.

Ève and I barely talked of any of this. We spent the whole of yesterday together hiking around the island. I showed her the flat rock where I like to sit and read. She showed me the cove next to her house, where she swims naked in the summertime. It's funny how there are still corners of this tiny island that even after so many years one or the other of us hasn't stumbled upon.

Then we went, like pilgrims, to the beach at La Roche-aux-Fras, which we found once again completely deserted. But it's true the tide was high and the Gouay under water, so there were no visitors apart from the tiny local population.

At one point as we were talking it occurred to me how extraordinary it is that she and I have lived for so long a few hundred meters apart, with no one else around, and yet we never developed even a polite neighborly relationship. It took these strange events to bring us together.

But it's not just that the circumstances were favorable or acted as a catalyst, as Ève candidly put it. "The truth is the last few years I turned into an insufferable misanthrope. What's happened now has reconciled me to the whole world. Even to the man who lives far too near me."

My only response to her teasing was to take her hand and not let it go. She went on talking. "The last few years the world has been no more than a battleground between greed and hatred. Everything has been spoiled: art, thought, writing, the future, sex, neighborliness. And now all of a sudden the slate has been wiped clean, history has begun anew, our planet has recovered its innocence. What do you think we should call it?"

"Our planet?" I asked, not fully paying attention to what she was saying.

"Our child."

The words and the tone in which they were spoken will echo in my head for a long while.

What had she said? Our child?

She sat down on a rock by the side of the path. I sat down beside her and looked at her. Was she laughing? She glanced away playfully, but I could see she was grinning.

I repeated what she'd said. "Our child?"

Instead of replying, she took my hands in hers and leaned her head against my chest.

My eyes were wet with tears.

We assumed they would come by sea, and for symbolic reasons would moor not far from where the attack on the floating hospital had taken place; or that they would arrive by air and disembark from a helicopter on the snowy lawn of Arlington Cemetery. But instead, they chose to come in through the back door, so to speak, discreetly joining the presidential motorcade in a black limousine. It was only at the last moment, when they were seen emerging from a vehicle and heading towards the official stands, that we realized they were there.

There were only two people in the delegation: up ahead walked Demosthenes, whom the security services recognized, which saved the representatives of Empedocles from having to declare their identities; and behind him a woman, clearly their leader.

Queen Electra.

Yesterday, no one knew her name or face, or even suspected her existence; today, she's the most famous, most photographed, and probably most powerful person on earth.

Queen Electra.

That's how she was dubbed, immediately, although no one knows her real title, or even if the political system that governs the intervening nation, as it is now known, has a monarch, a president, a prime minister, a satrap, or an archon at its head. Eventually we will find out, but today it doesn't matter. We needed to see a face, and we saw one.

Queen Electra.

The cameras could barely turn away from her. She

appeared constantly on screen, either in the center of the frame or to the side, in a separate frame altogether, as if we must not lose a single moment of her presence among us, not a glance, a nod, a shot of her fixed smile, the twitch of an eyelash.

I won't venture to guess her age or her ancestry. She could be forty, or twice that, and her physical traits could be associated with any continent: she has light-colored hair, a coppery complexion, high cheekbones, and sloping eyes. Didn't I once describe Agamemnon as resembling the love child of Sitting Bull and a Valkyrie? The same could be said of Electra, who looks as though she might, as in the classical myth, be his daughter, or at any rate related to him. I said that I used to find it hard to take my eyes off Agamemnon. How much more so with his queen.

Only a guest like her could compete for the limelight with Howard Milton. For if Electra's presence was miraculous, that of the president was no less so. In his recent public appearances, his face was like a death mask and his voice appropriately sepulchral. No longer. Moro's friend is young again. Scandalously young. His skin, his eyes, his bearing. The way he stood, sat, leaned towards Electra on his right, or Cynthia on his left. Happy to find himself in the center of such a trinity. Radiant, relaxed, splendid, triumphant.

We have to get used to the idea that after being treated with Empedocles's medicine, a person is not cured of a specific illness, but of all illness, visible or invisible, including those associated with aging. Now that they're "good as new," as the saying goes, a person can start living again as if the years they've already lived don't count anymore. I've experienced this myself, since going through the famous tunnel; I've observed it with delight in Ève; and now everyone in the whole world is witness to this eloquent example. How can we ever go back to the Before Times? How on earth can we go back to the days when disease and death were omnipotent?

When Milton came up to the podium, I was so fascinated by his appearance, his bearing, and the timbre of his voice, that it was an effort to focus on what he was saying. His speech was, however, the very opposite of banal:

> Today is both sad and auspicious. Sad, because the 123 people whose coffins are lined up here should never have died in this way. They should never have been targeted. They wanted to live, they had the right to live, and there can be no excuse for the cruel act that deprived them of that right.
>
> But today is also auspicious, because it allows us to ratify a serendipitous encounter with a precious branch of humanity. We had lost sight of our brothers and sisters, and we had lost our way. Today should be a day that allows us to reflect, and to ask ourselves, whoever we are, whatever country we come from, some fundamental questions: Who are we? Where are we going? What do we want to become? What kind of world do we wish to build? Based on what values?
>
> It is rare for us to ask ourselves such questions. We are usually so preoccupied with our daily

concerns, or, for leaders like me, focused on the day-to-day management of public affairs. But this encounter with our unexpected brothers should be an opportunity for us to take stock, to see where we have gone wrong and how we can turn things around.

The president went on to talk about some of the victims of the attack, including one of his young staffers who was killed with his mother while accompanying her to be treated on the hospital ship.

He went on to address the people of Empedocles directly:

Until now we have been on separate paths; from now on we shall have to walk alongside one another, with mutual respect, learning from each other, and feeling close to and in solidarity with each other for all time.

Know that you will always be welcome among us, and that together we will accomplish beautiful things.

It was Electra's turn to speak. Standing on the podium she placed her hands, one above the other, flat against the very upper part of her chest, almost at the base of her neck; an unusual posture, which looked to me—though this is mere supposition—like a sign of respect for the victims or for the audience. The silhouette she made was sculptural and graceful, and it's not impossible that the effect she sought was primarily aesthetic.

She began speaking in English, with a very slight

accent that I couldn't place. Swedish or Dutch, perhaps. She didn't read her speech, but nor did she seem to be extemporizing; it looked either as if she had memorized it, or she was reading from an invisible teleprompter.

Going against convention, she did not begin by addressing the president of the United States or anyone else in the audience. Instead she launched directly into the body of her speech.

> When in ancient times Empedocles climbed Mount Etna and felt the sulphury fumes and molten lava rising up from the bowels of the earth, he could have taken shelter, as wisdom demanded. But he continued walking until he found himself dangerously close to the crater.
>
> He knew he was risking death. We too, his far followers, know that if we approach the inferno, braving its flames with our bare hands, we might die. Death is our age-old enemy. We fight it as no one before us ever fought it. Sometimes we defeat it, sometimes it defeats us.
>
> Our enemy, did I say? I should have said it is our only enemy. For once we have acquired the wisdom and knowledge to turn back death, it becomes our only enemy. Until the end of time, it will be our only enemy, there is nothing else worth fighting for.
>
> For us, the friends of Empedocles, the case has already been made. And what about you, our newfound brothers? Are you ready to think of death as your only enemy? Yes, death, only death. Not rival powers, not other peoples, not other

*races. Not us. Only death. The single enemy worth
fighting, wrestling with, defeating. Are you ready
to reconsider your priorities, to open a new chapter, with us and with each other?*

She spoke these words and then fell silent, as if waiting for an answer. The silence went on so long that
President Milton was clearly beginning to wonder
whether he should stand up and respond. He was
glancing around, puzzled and even a little unset-
tled. But with a mischievous smile, Electra began to
speak again:

*We don't expect an answer today. We have spent
the last few weeks neutralizing the worst of the
weapons of mass destruction, which means that
now all of us can think calmly instead of making
hasty decisions. Take the time you need to come
to a decision, but never forget your friends are
here, watching and waiting.*

After she finished speaking, she stepped down from
the podium and returned to her seat to the right of
the president.

Like billions of my contemporaries, no doubt, I was
riveted the whole way through the ceremony. I sat
between Ève and Adrienne, both equally attentive
and absorbed. We all had the feeling we were wit-
nessing an unparalleled historical event, and none
of us wanted to say anything that might spoil the
solemnity of the moment.

It was only after the queen had fallen silent that

my goddaughter permitted herself to speak. "I thought we were waiting for them. Apparently, they are waiting for us," she observed shrewdly. "But I don't quite understand what we're supposed to do."

"Become adults, finally," Ève replied, as if she'd been mandated to answer on their behalf. "That's the condition for their return."

"Or it's a polite way of saying they aren't coming back," I said.

I expected vehement reactions from the two women. But neither protested. Whatever they have claimed over the last few days, it's clear they're both resigned to never seeing them again. It was just bravado that made my neighbor say, "They'll always be close to us, just as the sea is close."

She stared pensively out towards the horizon.

After Adrienne had gone up to bed, Ève turned to me and said, as though picking up the conversation of the day before, "If it's a girl, let's call her Electra."

I still couldn't wrap my brain around the idea of having a child. I asked her, with a sideways glance, as if checking whether she was serious or not, "Are you absolutely sure?" She gave an airy shrug.

"I'm not going to give you the details of my calendar, but the answer is yes, I am absolutely sure. Our child will be born next summer, by which time the friends of Empedocles will be back."

Thursday, December 9th

It's been exactly one month since this story— and this diary—began. More than once I've thought of giving up, but then something would happen that convinced me to carry on.

Now I'm going to put it away it for good, for there's no reason for me to keep it anymore. My home became an observation post for a while, but that's over now. Whether there's some kind of plot twist still to come, whether or not they return, this chapter is closed and my role as chronicler is over. Today I'm going to pick up my brushes and Indian ink and start working again.

I must add, however, by way of a personal epilogue, that the events of the last thirty days have not only changed the world and reset the historical record; they have also changed this island. It used to be a fortress of solitude, but now it's something else, for Ève and for me.

Will we soon be holding our own Queen Electra in our arms? I'd never have believed that at my age, and with my way of life, I'd become a father. For Ève it seemed even more improbable. But here we are. The intervening nation has, in a way, given us this child; and many years to see it grow up.

For this reason alone, though I have cursed them so often, I must bless our unexpected brothers.

NATASHA LEHRER is a prizewinning writer, translator, and editor. Her long-form journalism and book reviews have appeared in the *Guardian*, the *Observer*, the *Times Literary Supplement*, *The Nation*, *Haaretz*, and *Fantastic Man*, among others, and she is literary editor of the *Jewish Quarterly*. She has contributed to several books, including a chapter on France in *Looking for an Enemy: 8 Essays on Antisemitism*, edited by Jo Glanville (Norton, 2022). The writers she has translated include Nathalie Léger, Chantal Thomas, Vanessa Springora, Victor Segalen, Robert Desnos, and Georges Bataille. Her translations have been shortlisted and longlisted for several translation prizes, and in 2016 she was awarded the Scott Moncrieff prize for *Suite for Barbara Loden*.

Book Club Discussion Guides on our website.

World Editions promotes voices from around the globe by publishing books from many different countries and languages in English translation. Through our work, we aim to enhance dialogue between cultures, foster new connections, and open doors which may otherwise have remained closed.

On the Design

As book design is an integral part of the reading experience, we would like to acknowledge the work of those who shaped the form in which the story is housed.

Tessa van der Waals (Netherlands) is responsible for the cover design, cover typography, and art direction of all World Editions books. She works in the internationally renowned tradition of Dutch Design. Her bright and powerful visual aesthetic maintains a harmony between image and typography, and captures the unique atmosphere of each book. She works closely with internationally celebrated photographers, artists, and letter designers. Her work has frequently been awarded prizes for Best Dutch Book Design.

The cover image was created by Basia Stryjecka, a graphic designer and artist from the American Midwest. With a strong interest in color, composition, and texture, Basia Stryjecka applies a deep knowledge of design to her abstract work. Her goal is to bring a sense of play, texture, and creativity to her design projects. The particular image used here is named Modern Abstract Landscapes. The cover font is Plakato Paper Rough, a multi-layered font designed by Bas Jacobs, the designer of Dolly, also used for the interior. Plakato is a stencil love affair – a family of display fonts consisting of various eye-catching styles, each of them very bold.

Euan Monaghan (United Kingdom) is responsible for the typography and careful interior book design.

The text on the inside covers and the press quotes are set in Circular, designed by Laurenz Brunner (Switzerland) and published by Swiss type foundry Lineto.

All World Editions books are set in the typeface Dolly, specifically designed for book typography. Dolly creates a warm page image perfect for an enjoyable reading experience. This typeface is designed by Underware, a European collective formed by Bas Jacobs (Netherlands), Akiem Helmling (Germany), and Sami Kortemäki (Finland). Underware are also the creators of the World Editions logo, which meets the design requirement that "a strong shape can always be drawn with a toe in the sand."